A MESSAGE FROM CHICKEN HOUSE

I love old – or rather 'vintage' – clothes. Familiar, comfortable and satisfyingly worn in, these beauties can be mixed and matched or combined with new purchases to create your very own style – they're a link between past and future. But Laurel Remington's new hero, Andy, doesn't agree ... not at first anyway. Can old clothes really change her life? Find out in this original, heart-warming and huggable new story from the lovely author of *The Secret Cooking Club*.

BARRY CUNNINGHAM
Publisher
Chicken House

The POLKA DOT SHOP

LAUREL REMINGTON

Chicken House

2 Palmer Street, Frome, Somerset BA11 1DS
www.chickenhousebooks.com

Text © Laurel Remington 2018

First published in Great Britain in 2018
Chicken House
2 Palmer Street
Frome, Somerset BA11 1DS
United Kingdom
www.chickenhousebooks.com

Cover and interior design by Helen Crawford-White
Typeset by Dorchester Typesetting Group Ltd
Printed and bound in Great Britain by CPI Group (UK) Ltd, Croydon CR0 4YY

The paper used in this Chicken House book is made
from wood grown in sustainable forests.

1 3 5 7 9 10 8 6 4 2

British Library Cataloguing in Publication data available.

PB ISBN 978-1-911077-75-6
eISBN 978-1-911490-55-5

For Eve, Rose and Grace

Distrust any enterprise
that requires new clothes.

~ Henry David Thoreau,
Walden

RICHES TO RAGS

On the worst day of my life, the school announced a new policy – no more uniforms! You would think we'd won a war or something – everybody rushed out to the playing field at break time, yelling and cheering. Then kids started stripping off their brown blazers, striped ties and burgundy jumpers and making a big pile. Pretty soon everyone was jumping on the pile like a giant beanbag, and a couple of the boys started taking off more of their clothes – until a teacher came and put a stop to it.

I stood by the door to my classroom, pulling my blazer tightly around my chest. For me it was protection, and I didn't want to let it go. The idea behind the policy was that 'the children of Green-hill School should have the right to express themselves through their choices of clothing, hairstyle and accessories'. I guess it sounded good on paper, and it was great for most of the kids.

But not for me.

The school sent home a letter to the parents about the new policy. I threw it in a bin on my way home. For the next three weeks, I was the only kid who showed up in full uniform. I was only eleven at the time, so the kids weren't as mean then as they are now. Still, there was whispering behind hands when I entered the classroom, and my best friend, Olivia, became the centre of a new crowd – the girls whose mums took them on shopping trips at the weekend.

At first, I joined in as they sat around a table at lunchtime, oohing and aahing over Chloe's sequin top and appliqué denim jacket from River Island, Alexandra's stripy jersey dress and navy wedges from Debenhams, and Sophie's silver knit cardigan with the British flag buttons from Zara Kids. By the end of the first week, I was tired of pretending that Mum was 'too busy' to take me shopping, so I started going to the library at lunchtime to do my homework.

At the end of the third week, my English

teacher, Ms Tripp, drew me aside. 'Are you OK, Andy?' she'd asked, glancing down at my greyish-tinged white blouse that accidentally got washed with black socks.

'Yeah, I'm fine — thanks,' I'd said. It was safer that way.

Maybe it was Ms Tripp who decided that what I wore to 'express myself' was her business, and it shouldn't include my old school uniform. Because someone called Mum and told her about the new policy. When I got home that night, she greeted me at the door with a huge bag and a: 'You must be so excited — I've brought you some fun clothes from the shop that I just know will be perfect for you.'

Mum's shop. *Eliza's Emporium.* There's a motto painted on the door: 'Vintage and Pre-loved Clothing, New to U!' When I saw that bag, my stomach plummeted, and I knew then that no blazer and burgundy jumper could protect me from what was to come.

And they didn't.

Mum's idea of 'perfect for me' was a pink Hello Kitty T-shirt with the rubbery white stuff on the face starting to peel off like the cat had really bad eczema. That and a pair of black leggings, which might have been OK if they hadn't ended ten centimetres short of my ankles and had crocheted lace at the bottom. She'd also brought a pair of pink Converse trainers that were two sizes too big. Even though they'd been through the washing machine, I swear I could still smell someone else's sweaty feet, and they made me feel like I was some kind of clown who'd escaped from a really scary circus. To top it all off there was a cropped pink jacket made of some kind of fake fur that felt like matted Barbie Doll hair.

I really didn't want to hurt Mum's feelings, but when I saw those clothes, I felt like crying. For one thing, I am not a *pink* kind of girl, but I guess Mum didn't know that because I always wore my school uniform during the week, and at the weekends I tended to be in my pyjamas a lot. (My pyjamas were red with white polka dots on them, and were a Christmas gift from my Aunt Linda who lives in the Lake District. They were really warm and lovely. I wish they still fit me.) But the main thing is, I really hate the idea of wearing someone else's cast-off old clothes all the time.

'Um, thanks, Mum,' I'd said, swallowing hard. She must have thought I was overcome with joy or something, because she pulled me into her arms, and told me that this was going to be 'such fun!'

Yeah.

When I went to school that first day, I went into the loos to check my reflection in the mirror, hoping that the outfit wasn't as bad as I thought. As I was standing there, Olivia and Sophie came in.

Olivia looked at my outfit, then at Sophie, then back at me. 'When did you get a dog, Andy?' she said.

'I don't . . . we don't have a dog.'

Olivia snickered and pointed at one of my matted pink cuffs. 'Then what tried to kill and eat that jacket?'

She and Sophie burst out laughing. I was kind of shocked. I mean, Olivia was my friend. So I'd thought, anyway.

For a while after that happened, I would get dressed in the mornings in whatever Mum had brought me (I did finally tell her *no more pink*), then when I got to school I changed in the loos into a pair of leggings, a T-shirt and a really long grey jumper (another gift from Aunt Linda) that I'd already worn so often that it had holes in the elbows and cuffs. But then I overheard Olivia whispering to Chloe that it looked like I was wearing something from her grandma's 'rag bag', whatever that is, and then Chloe started calling me 'Rags' and the name stuck for the whole term. Eventually people got bored of it, but sometimes I still feel like it's who I am.

Now fast forward two years – last week I had my thirteenth birthday. You've probably guessed that Olivia is no longer my friend – nor are Alexandra, Chloe, Sophie or any of the girls in that crowd. Their mums take them to the big Westfield shopping centre in town every week-end, and at lunchtime they're constantly looking at fashion magazines and browsing shop websites on their phones. But while I'm still a little jealous (OK, a lot jealous) of their lovely brand-new clothes, I don't really miss *them* that much. For one thing, they still act like they're the fashion police – they lurk in the loos at break time, and everyone who walks in either gets the 'oh, that top is cute' thumbs up, or, more likely, a 'did your granny die in that dress?' or 'did you borrow those jeans from a homeless person?' thumbs down. It's stupid, and it's mean, and I'm glad I'm not part of it. The other reason I don't mind not hanging out with them any more is because after the whole eating-lunch-by-myself-and-going-to-the-library thing, I made two new friends.

The first is Carrie. I met her in the canteen when we were both trying to sit by ourselves and there weren't enough tables. I guess she wanted to be alone because a lot of the kids called her 'Fat Girl' (which is just *so* original, isn't it?). We ended up sitting together at opposite ends of the one empty table a few days in a row. It was kind of fascinating to watch her eat her lunch. She would always start with a big Tupperware of salad heaped with soggy lettuce, bleeding beetroot and sweetcorn, which she'd brought especially from home, and she'd always have a tiny plate of chips on the side from the canteen. I watched her push the vegetables around with her fork, trying to make herself eat a bite, and then rewarding herself with a chip. At the moment when that chip went in her mouth, her face looked like heaven.

One day, I couldn't stand it any more. I watched the struggle for a while and then went back to the queue and got a big plate of chips. I came back to the table and set them down between us. I took one, looking at her all the while I chewed and swallowed it.

'Thanks,' she said. She ate one of them, and I ate one, then one more, and together we finished all of them.

Now we're good friends. I try to protect her from people being mean – the next time someone called her 'Fat Girl' in the canteen, I told him that 'Carrie can lose weight but you'll always be stupid.' He'd laughed in my face but he'd turned the brightest shade of red.

My other friend is Alice, but only the teachers call her that. Everyone else calls her 'Stevie', after Stephen Hawking, because she uses a wheelchair. She used to walk, but then she was in a car accident when she was eight years old. The doctor says she might be able to walk again some day, but she'll have to learn all over again like a toddler. She doesn't like the chair – obviously – but she loves the nickname. I'm sure someone probably made it up to tease her, but instead of letting it bother her she decided to live up to it. She was already really into science anyway, and now her dream is to go to Oxford or Cambridge and study physics as a tribute to her hero, Stephen Hawking. She knows about all kinds of stuff like black holes, dark matter, wormholes and the heat death of the universe. She also has every episode of both *Star Trek: The Next Generation* and *Doctor Who* on DVD at her house, and watches all kinds of new sci-fi programmes on Netflix.

Carrie and I got to know her when she came to our school after we started sitting together in the canteen. Because there were only the two of us at the table, there was room for Stevie to roll up in her wheelchair and join us. Sometimes I'm almost grateful that the school ruined my life, because I now have two friends who are a lot nicer and more interesting than the old crowd.

Almost.

Because the truth is, even two years later, I still have a major hang-up about the whole clothes thing. I know it sounds really shallow, but on the rare occasions when Mum and I go into town and I pass the shop windows, I feel like I could kill for a little stripy summer dress from Zara; sell a kidney for the sparkly sequin plimsolls at New Look. And I'd definitely trade Mum's shop for just about anything from Topshop.

Mum still loves bringing me home all kinds of clothes, none of which ever seem to fit me quite right – all baggy button-down shirts, faded T-shirts, calf-length dresses in ugly floral prints, bobbled cardigans and tatty jeans (don't even get me started on the jeans). It should be fine – I mean, not everyone in school is a fashion plate – far from it. I'm not the only one who regularly gets the thumbs down from the fashion police, and sometimes I've even worn something that got the thumbs up.

But no matter what my clothes look like, the problem is that I know they come from Mum's shop. Nothing ever has that new-shop smell, a crisp cardboard tag; that stiff, starchy texture that means no one else has worn it. Ever. Anything that comes from Mum's shop is 'pre-owned', 'pre-loved', second-hand, *used*.

I wasn't going to mention this, but I really need to get it off my chest. It's a horrible secret that I haven't told anyone before – not even Carrie and Stevie. I like to think that maybe if I don't say it or think about it, it will turn out not to be true.

So here goes: Mum even brings me pre-owned *underwear* from the shop.

Can you think of anything grosser; more disgusting; more downright soul-destroying than wearing someone else's cast-off bras and knickers? Mum says that it's no big deal – that once something's washed, it doesn't matter that someone else has worn it. She says that lots of the bras and pants that come into the shop are practically new – someone's grandma bought her Minnie Mouse knickers when she wanted *Frozen*, or green when she wanted pink. I don't bother to point out that at age thirteen, I hardly want to be wearing Minnie Mouse knickers, or any knickers at all that someone else has worn.

So here's another secret. When I turned twelve, I took some money from the biscuit tin in the kitchen. I told Mum I was going over to Stevie's but instead I took the bus into town. I went to M&Co and bought myself a new white bra and a six-pack of cotton knickers. I've been wearing them non-stop for the last year (washing them regularly, of course, in the sink). When Mum does laundry once a week, I throw the awful second-hand knickers into the laundry basket and Mum's none the wiser. I wouldn't want to hurt her feelings . . .

Because here's the thing: I love Mum. She's a really cool person. Everyone who meets her thinks so. She's the kind of mum who doesn't nag at me to do my homework or tidy my room. The kind who orders in a pizza once a week on Friday nights; and lets me keep the light on late when I'm reading a good book. She's been on her own ever since my dad died when I was four, and I'm really proud of the way she works hard with the shop to make ends meet and get by. So I really don't have any problems with her – except for my one BIG problem.

I know it's wrong to be vain about things like hair and clothes and how you look, and which boys fancy you and which girls want to be your friend. And it's a good thing I'm not vain, because I have nothing to be vain about. I'm tall and skinny, without much of a chest or hips. If I had to name my one best feature it would be my hair, which is long and brown and goes almost down to my waist. My eyes are brown and I have long eyelashes. Stevie and Carrie say that I'm lucky – that I'll never have to wear mascara. They don't know how lucky I really am, because sometimes people donate old make-up to mum's shop and people do actually buy it. I'm sure I saw something in a magazine once that said that make-up can carry *E.coli*. Using someone else's mascara could probably make you go blind. So it's good that I don't need it. Buying used make-up is almost as bad as wearing someone else's knickers. But not quite.

Mum is one of those people who lives for the whole vintage thing. Before she met my dad, she went to fashion college in London, and for a while she wanted to be a teacher. My dad was a news photographer, and when they were first together they travelled the world to places like India and Thailand. When Mum got pregnant with me, they settled down in the village where Dad grew up and Mum opened the shop. Then Dad died. It wasn't a glamorous death like being killed in a war zone, or getting eaten by something in the jungle. He had a weak heart and collapsed while he was taking out the rubbish. I don't really remember him except some snippets and images – strong hands; a man with blond hair lifting me on to his shoulders. Mum says I was too young to remember him at all, but I don't think I could have made those things up.

Like me, Mum's tall and thin; but unlike me, old clothes from the sixties and seventies and even the eighties look good on her. She knows how to accessorize – which plastic bracelets go with a sixties floral miniskirt; or which baggy 'layered look' jumper is going to look good over someone's 'lived-in' Levi 501 jeans.

Mum always says that vintage is a 'state of mind'. It's definitely got my mind in a state.

Anyway, so that's my story – riches to Rags. Did I mention that I just turned thirteen? I'm a teenager now, and I've seriously had enough.

But what can I do?

2

THE STREET THAT TIME FORGOT

It's a week after my birthday. After school, I walk to *Eliza's Emporium*. It's at the opposite end of the high street from school. On the way I pass the church, a bookshop, a bakery (my stomach rumbles every time I walk past), a chemist and a couple of other shops selling knick-knacks and stationery. It's a nice quiet little village, close enough to transport so that well-off families like Olivia's and Chloe's live there – with mums or dads who commute to London. The high street leads to a small village green where there's a war memorial and a cricket pitch, and then starts again on the other side.

Unfortunately, the *Eliza's Emporium* end of the

high street is nothing like the nice end. Just off the green, there's a garage, a betting shop and a funeral parlour. Next to that is a chippie called *Mr Chips*. Beyond that is an old theatre that's been boarded up for years, and on the other side of that is *Eliza's Emporium*. Mum doesn't mind the fact that her shop's not at the posh end. I've heard her telling people that the shop is in an 'up and coming' area, and I guess she's right – the only way *is* up.

I try to avoid looking at the window of *Eliza's Emporium*, but my eye is drawn to it, the way people slow down to look at a car accident. This month Mum has done it up with some of her favourite stock – the wedding dresses. There are two full-sized mannequins with a little pink and white child's tea set on a table between them. The mannequins are wearing lacy, fluffy, satin wedding dresses, veils and white shoes. Their plastic faces are frozen in painted-on smiles. To me, they look like corpses – pale, dead and still. Or maybe like the character Miss Havisham in *Great Expectations* – she was jilted by her lover and wore her wedding dress until it practically fell to pieces off her body.

I stare at the display wondering who would buy someone else's used wedding dress? To me, it just seems so wrong. I mean, you don't know anything about the bride who wore the dress before – was she happy? Sad? A good person? An axe murderess? Anything is possible. Yet Mum loves it when she gets wedding dresses to sell in the shop. People do buy them – and here's the really scary thing: a lot of *men* buy them. (Mum says it's mostly for stag dos and fancy dress parties – but it's just *so* creepy.)

The little bell on the door tinkles as I push it open. I take a deep breath of outside air – car exhaust, deep fried fish – because I don't like the smell inside Mum's shop. It's a mixture of different laundry detergents, floral perfumes, the sandalwood room freshener sticks that Mum keeps by the till, and underneath it all the smell of old lady. I don't know why the shop smells the way it does, or why it bothers me and no one else.

There's no one sitting on the stool behind the glass display counter where the gaudy costume jewellery is kept, and the till is sat. 'Hello?' I hear Mum call out from the back stockroom. The single word has a lilt to it, like I might be a 'mad-for-vintage' customer who will stay all afternoon, drink lemon and ginger tea, try things on in the fitting room and talk sixties fashion or something.

'Hi, Mum,' I call out, hoping she won't be too disappointed that it's just me and not her dream customer. I sit down on the stool and look around the shop.

Every inch of floor and wall space is crammed with stuff. There are long racks of dresses and coats on two walls and down the middle of the room; a shoe rack at the back next to the door to the stockroom is overflowing with tatty old heels and trainers. Above the racks is a row of shelving with handbags and tall boots on it. And then there's Mum's 'special display stock'. One mannequin (head and torso only, no legs) is wearing a lilac and pink flower print dress, lots of pearl beads and some kind of feather thing in her hair that Mum calls a 'fascinator'; another one is wearing a hideous gold lamé prom dress; and the worst one of all has a coconut bra, a dusty plastic flower lei and a Hawaiian grass skirt around its hips. Awful.

The walls are painted different colours – sky blue, yellow, green, and there's a dressing room in the back stockroom with an Indian print curtain. There's a single light in the centre of the ceiling – a brass and crystal chandelier that is draped with old scarves and men's ties. The shop is so cluttered and higgledy-piggledy that I feel a little dizzy just being here.

If I were in charge, I'd get a roll of bin bags and clear everything out. Start again from scratch. But

Mum would never do anything like that. She knows and loves every single piece of clothing that's here. If any of it has a story, she knows it.

There's the sound of rushing footsteps from the back of the shop. 'Hi, Andy.' Mum comes towards me in a waft of sandalwood and rose. She's wearing a billowy tie-dyed dress, silver Roman sandals, a necklace made from big seeds, and bangles that clink on her wrist as she sweeps me into a hug. On her, all that stuff together kind of works. Jumbled together on a rack (and on most other people), it just doesn't.

'Jolanta and I are in the back sorting through some new stock,' she says. 'Do you want to come and see? There's some great stuff.'

I loosen myself from her grip, trying not to seem like I'm pulling away.

'Sorry, Mum,' I say. 'I've got maths to finish up so I thought I'd go over to Stevie's house. Is that OK? I'll have dinner there.'

'Oh, right,' Mum says. 'OK.' Her eyes are big and brown, just like mine. I recognize the look in them − or rather, I don't recognize it. Lately, Mum's happy, bubbly personality has started to seem like an act. Once, late at night, I woke up and heard a noise coming from her bedroom. It sounded like crying. I put the pillow over my head and shoved tissues in my ears. Mum never cries. Nothing ever bothers her. But something must be . . .

I know I should ask her – try to help her out if I can. But to be honest, I just don't really know where to start. For so many years Mum and I were really close. And then the whole school uniform thing happened, and ever since then I feel like we've been at opposite ends of a rope bridge over a river that keeps getting wider.

I guess most of it is my fault. As much as I've tried to keep from her the fact that I don't like the clothes from the shop, I know she suspects. She's stopped bringing me so much stuff, and has tried to get me to come in and pick out things myself. Usually, I find an excuse not to. I also haven't told her about the fashion police at school. I know she'd just say some kind of 'Mum thing', like they're jealous of me (as if!) or that I have my 'own style' and shouldn't let other people's opinions bother me. But she's not the one who has to deal with it.

'OK then,' I say. 'I mean . . . I'll see you later.' I hover for a second, hating the fact that I'm probably disappointing her by not showing more of an interest in the shop. But in truth, I just want to be out of there.

'Of course, darling. You go and have a good time with your friends.'

'Thanks.' I take a breath. 'Um, Mum, are you OK? You look a little bit—'

'Liza? Do you need help?'

Jolanta, Mum's assistant, comes through the curtain in the back, sewing scissors in her hand. Jolanta's eighteen and came over from Poland a few years ago to learn English. She works three afternoons a week in the shop, and the other days she goes to fashion college. At the weekend she and her friends sell their work at a market stall. She's really focused on becoming a clothing designer, and I hope she does – the sooner the better. For some reason, we've never really got on. I have this sneaking suspicion that sometimes Mum's asked Jolanta her opinion about some of the clothes she's brought home for me. I have this picture in my mind of Jolanta finding some of the worst old tat and sticking it in a bag and saying it would be perfect for me.

'Hey, Jolanta,' I say. 'You OK?'

'Hi, Andy,' she says flatly. Then she turns to Mum. 'Guess what, Liza?' she says, much more animated. 'There are some decent labels in that house clearance bag. I found a Phase Eight tunic and a Wallis cardigan. The tunic has a little stain, but

I'm sure you can get it out with some vinegar.'

'Great.' Mum's face lights up. 'I'd love to see.' She hovers for a moment like *she* feels obligated to stick around and chat to me. But I know she really wants to look at the stuff that Jolanta's found.

My cue to leave. 'Bye, Mum,' I say, 'I won't be late.'

'OK, Andy . . .' She gives me another quick hug. 'I love you.'

'Me too.'

3

AT THE CHIPPIE

Outside the shop I gasp in a breath of outside air. My heart is beating quickly, and I'm glad to be out of there. I know it's stupid to let the state of the shop bother me so much. And Mum ... and Jolanta ... that smell ... all that stuff ...

I walk slowly down the pavement past the old theatre. Beneath the graffiti and plywood boards I can make out the shredded edges of old posters of bands and dance acts that once performed there. I wonder why someone doesn't just tear the theatre down and build something new. That's what I would do if it were up to me. Tear down the whole block and start again – make it into something nice like the other end of the high street.

Except, not the chippie. That could stay.

I pass the theatre and stop outside *Mr Chips*. The smell of deep-fried fish and chips, salt and vinegar, is enough to get the smell of Mum's shop out of my nose; the sizzle of oil and clanging dishes loud enough to drown out my thoughts. I go inside to buy some drinks to take to Stevie's.

Usually there's a queue for fish and chips here – construction workers, families, commuters, old people – and with good reason. The fish and chips here really are to die for. There's a board up on the wall saying that they use only sustainable fish, low-fat oil, sea salt and organic potatoes. I guess that kind of thing really does make a difference.

Today though, the shop is empty except for a couple of sixth formers sitting at a table by the window, and two men in Royal Mail uniforms sitting nearer the counter.

I go to the cooler and grab three cans of Diet Coke, and go up to the counter. The owner is wiping down the glass case with a cloth. His real name isn't Mr Chips (obviously), but Mr LeBoeff. He looks like he's a few years older than Mum, and has black hair with a sprinkling of grey at the sides. He has a nice face – friendly, but somehow I always think he looks a bit sad. It's ironic that his name sounds almost exactly like 'The Beef' in

French (according to Stevie), and that's not on the menu here.

'And how are you today, Andrea?' he says, giving me a friendly smile.

'Fine, thanks.' I'm in here quite often, but it still catches me off guard that anyone would call me by my real name. But maybe the French are more formal than we are. I've often wondered how he ended up here, running a British fish and chip joint. But even though he's friendly and chatty whenever I come in, I've never got up the courage to ask him.

He hands me the drinks in a brown paper bag. As I'm paying for them, a door bangs open at the back and Mr LeBoeff's nephew walks in. Immediately I'm struck dumb and can't move. He's Just. So. Gorgeous. His dark hair falls in a curtain over the side of his face, and his eyes are greyish blue. His fingers are long like he should be playing the piano instead of frying fish. He's a little shorter than I am, but I guess no one's perfect.

'Ah, Thomas.' Mr LeBoeff says, smiling broadly. When he says the name with his accent it sounds cool and French like To-MAS. 'How was school today, boy?'

Thomas looks at me as he puts on his white apron. I lean forward like a plant growing towards the light. But I can't tell if his gaze is friendly or not. We've never really spoken, other than him sometimes taking my order or asking if I want salt and vinegar. I do know that he's a year older than me and goes to the local Catholic school. They still wear uniforms there. I've seen him waiting for the bus in a neat grey jumper and black trousers, and I've envied the girls who go to that school with him. But I've also seen him around in a black leather biker jacket and jeans, looking like a model or a member of a boy band. In general, he makes me feel very nervous, and I'm not sure if it's in a good or a bad way.

'It was fine,' he says.

Mr LeBoeff turns back to me, grinning from ear to ear. 'Thomas wants to be an architect,' he says proudly.

'That's nice,' I say.

Thomas frowns like he's embarrassed. 'We're almost out of potatoes. I'll go down to the cellar for some more.'

'You see – he's too modest,' Mr LeBoeff says.

'Um, yeah.' I take the paper bag off the counter and turn to leave.

'And how is your mum?' he says.

I'm sure he's just being friendly, but something in his voice makes me pause. I look at him – his brow is furled like he's concerned.

'She's fine,' I say. 'Why?'

'It's just that she has not stopped by lately. I wondered how she's doing.'

'Fine.' I frown as the word comes out of my mouth. 'Just fine.'

I go out the door, closing it hard behind me. Mum *is* fine. Why wouldn't she be? And what business is it of his anyway?

4

A REALLY BAD IDEA

I forget all about Mr LeBoeff and even his gorgeous nephew – better not to think about *him* ever – and spend a fun evening with Stevie and Carrie. We do our homework, watch two episodes of a new series called *Galactic X*; and then, while Stevie and Carrie go to the kitchen to make popcorn, I browse the latest Asos collection on Stevie's iPad. I find the most adorable little print skirt: brown corduroy with circles sewed on to it in different pastel colours. Even on sale, it's £19. I don't have that kind of money.

But as I browse the designs, feeling my usual resentment that Mum's shop doesn't sell anything cool or hip – unless you count things that might have been cool or hip thirty years ago — an idea strikes me. Something that's so obvious that I feel like an idiot for never thinking of it before.

I could get a job. I could babysit or deliver leaflets or flip burgers — anything to make a little pocket money. Except, would anyone hire a thirteen-year-old? Is it even legal?

'What are you looking at?' Carrie comes in with two bowls of popcorn. She hands me one.

'Oh, nothing — you know . . . just stuff.'

'I bet it's clothes — AGAIN!' Stevie wheels over with a bowl of popcorn in her lap.

'OK,' I confess. 'You're right. Isn't this the cutest skirt ever?' I hand her the screen.

'You'd look great in that,' Stevie says. 'Or just about anything. I mean, you're so tall.'

'Thanks,' I say. 'But I can't afford it.'

Carrie looks over Stevie's shoulder. 'It *is* cute,' she says. 'But there must be some cute skirts in your mum's shop too.'

I sigh. 'You just don't *get* it.'

'I think we do,' Stevie says. She flicks a piece of popcorn at me. 'You're a snob. You only want to wear clothes that are brand-new.'

'I am *not* a snob!' I flick the piece back. 'I just don't like having to wear people's stinky old cast-offs all the time.'

Carrie shrugs. 'I think your mum's shop is cool,' she says. 'It has character.'

'I like that,' Stevie says. 'Character.'

'It may have character, but it ought to have some decent stuff to sell,' I say. I suddenly remember what Mr LeBoeff said about his nephew wanting to be an architect. 'When I'm grown up, I'm going to have a shop too. But I'm only going to sell top-end, high-quality designer stuff.'

'Maybe I can be your plus-size model,' Carrie says. She launches a piece of popcorn at me. 'They have them, you know.'

'Since when have you been interested in fashion?'

'Since always – can't you tell?' Carrie struts forward in her baggy flannel shirt and boy jeans. I clap in rhythm, and Stevie laughs and showers her with a handful of popcorn.

Carrie sits down on the sofa, picking up the stray popcorn and shoving it in her mouth. 'What about you, Einstein?' she says to Stevie. 'What do you want to do – discover a new elementary particle or something?'

'No.' Stevie smiles assuredly. 'I'm going to be an astronaut – like Tim Peake. Up in space, I'd just float so I won't need to walk.' She shrugs. 'And I'd have lots of time on my hands to discover a new elementary particle.'

'Here's one for you!' I pelt her with popcorn.

Stevie leans forward and retaliates, showering Carrie and me with popcorn, salt and kernels. There's popcorn everywhere and we're laughing at nothing, but it's really funny anyway.

There's the sound of a car in the drive – Stevie's mum coming home from work.

The three of us look at each other, swallowing back a few stray smirks. Then Carrie and I get down on our hands and knees and sweep up the popcorn with our hands. When all of it is back in the bowls, I straighten up.

'I don't have a clue what I'll end up doing when I'm older, but I'm thinking about trying to get a job now to earn some money,' I announce.

'A job?' Stevie looks shocked. 'What about school?'

'Who's going to hire you?' Carrie adds.

'I don't know.' To be honest, I was hoping they would be a little more encouraging. 'But I'm sure I could do something. After school, and on the weekends. Like babysitting or maybe delivering leaflets.'

'It's pretty obvious what you can do, isn't it?' Stevie says.

'What?'

'You can work at your mum's shop.'

'The *Emporium*?' My stomach clenches. 'No, I couldn't.'

Carrie waves her hand in front of me like a hypnotist's crystal. 'Think of the skirt, think of the skirt ...'

'No skirt is THAT cute!'

'Come on, Andy ...' Stevie's voice is level. 'You love clothes; your mum has a clothes shop. It's a no-brainer. You can learn what it's like to run a shop. And who knows? Maybe you'll find some hidden gems.'

I shudder as all the things Mum's brought me over the years flash before my eyes. The tatty tops, the faded jeans, the second-hand underwear. I think of the fashion police at school and how much it hurt when they called me 'Rags', even though I knew it was just a name and wasn't really *me* at all. I know my friends are trying to be help-ful, and maybe I do sound like a snob. But until they've walked a mile in my too-big 'pre-loved' trainers, they'll never really understand.

'Well, give it some thought.' Stevie gives me an encouraging smile.

'Yeah,' I say non-committally. 'Anyway, I should probably go home. I don't want Mum to get worried.' I stand up and grab my rucksack.

'Hey, are you OK?' Carrie calls out.

I don't answer as I close the door behind me and go out into the night.

It's later than I thought. Outside, a sliver of moon has risen above the houses as I walk to the end of Stevie's road and turn on to the high street. I wish I'd never mentioned the idea of getting a job — wish it hadn't even crossed my mind. Because deep down, I know that Stevie's right. If I really want to earn some money, then working at Mum's shop *is* a no-brainer. Thomas isn't that much older than me, and he has a job — but only at his uncle's shop. Who else besides Mum is going to hire me? But I just hate the idea of being there surrounded by all that stuff.

The shops are dark as I walk past. Even the chippie is shut, and that stays open until ten. The street lights seem dimmer than usual. The cold air is sharp through the holes in my jumper and I start to shiver a little.

As I pass the old theatre next to Mum's shop, I stop walking. Behind the boarded-up windows, yellow light is spilling out around the edges. I'm surprised that the place has electricity — no one has been inside for years that I know of. But now, someone is. From inside I hear a faint noise like music. A radio? My heart begins to speed up. Who's inside – a homeless person? A burglar?

I walk on past the theatre and peer inside the window of Mum's shop. Even in the dark, the painted-on doll's eyes of the mannequin in the wedding dress stare back at me. If she's seen anything, she's not saying. The whole thing gives me the creeps. I walk home quickly, glancing over my shoulder at no one and nothing.

In the night, my dreams are scary and real. I'm walking through a beautiful clothing store, taking loads of things off the racks to try on: the corduroy skirt, a silver dress, a cute stripy top, starched new jeans . . . but as I'm walking to the fitting room, a line of mannequins with painted-on faces strut out towards me to the sound of a radio. They're wearing old jeans, raggedy wedding dresses and a grass skirt with Minnie Mouse pants underneath. Marching towards me, not stopping, they're going to trample me! I drop the armful of nice clothes and start to run—

I sit bolt upright in bed, my heart racing. The room is greyish in the dawn light. Everything is familiar – the shelves of books and my old stuffed toys, clothing strewn on the floor, my brown suede beanbag chair, the pink and white striped duvet. I laugh at myself for getting worked up about a dream. But I know what I have to do, and I'm going to do it.

As soon as I hear Mum coming out of her room, I get up and put on some of the latest clothes that Mum's brought me: a pair of faded Fair Isle print leggings that someone donated to the shop after Christmas, and a 'matching' red T-shirt with DON'T WORRY, BE HAPPY printed on it along with a cheeky-faced emoji. On someone else, the T-shirt might be OK, but it's *so* not me. I shove my holey jumper in my bag to put over it.

I go into the kitchen so I can talk to Mum before she leaves to go to the shop. In between pouring some Weetabix into a bowl and buttering a piece of toast, she tells me off about coming home so late. I tell her that I'm sorry – I won't do it again – then tell her about the new show we watched, and about what I'm doing in school. I'm waffling, I realize. I know I should just come out with it, but I can't bring myself to say the words.

Mum slips into her habit of talking about a new batch of clothes that came into the shop from the estate of some old lady who died. Apparently it included a bunch of clothes for a Scottie dog in six different tartan patterns. Half of me is listening and giving a few one- or two-word answers, the other half is trying to psych myself up. I can only eat a few bites of breakfast so I take my bowl to the sink and rinse it. Mum potters around getting ready to go to the shop, and I dawdle over getting my stuff ready for school. Finally, we're both ready to leave. It's now or never.

I pause at the door, rucksack slung over my shoulder. I need to get this over with before I can convince myself that it's A Really Bad Idea.

'Uh, Mum,' I say, 'can I talk to you about something?'

'Sure, Andy. What's up?'

'The thing is, Mum,' I say, 'I want to get a job.'

'A job?' She looks surprised. 'Like babysitting?'

I take a breath. 'Actually, I thought I could work at the shop.'

'The *Emporium*?' She frowns.

'Yeah.' I swallow hard. 'The *Emporium*.'

'And you want to be paid?'

'Well, yeah, that's the point.' I smile awkwardly. 'I want to earn some pocket money.' For new clothes and stuff, I don't add.

'It's a good idea,' Mum says hesitantly. 'And maybe we can talk about it again when you're a little older. But I don't think it would work right now.'

I lower my rucksack to the floor. I thought she'd be over the moon that I'm finally showing an interest in the shop. So why isn't she?

'I'm serious, Mum. I could do it – easy. You talk about the place all the time. You may not think I've listened, but I have.'

'I know, Andy. It's . . . it's not that. I just think that right now you need to focus on school. That's the most important thing.' She checks her watch. 'Now, I need to go, and so do you.'

'Will you at least think about it?'

'Of course.' She exhales in relief and I know she's lying.

5

THE WHITE BAG

Now that Mum's said no to me working at the shop, for the first time ever, I actually want to. I must know more about the shop than anyone else except Mum, and probably Jolanta. Night after night at dinner, for years and years, she's talked about *Eliza's Emporium*. I know loads – from when the tax returns are due, to how to get water stains out of a suede coat. I even kind of like it when Mum talks about fixing up her 'finds', as she calls them – repairing zips, adding colourful patches or funky buttons to things that come her way. I like seeing her happy.

And really, how bad would it be? As Stevie said, I could learn more about working in a shop even if second-hand clothes aren't my thing. I have to keep my eye on the prize – if I make some pocket money, then I can buy myself something new. The spring sales are coming soon – I've only got a few weeks to save up.

After school, I go directly to *Eliza's Emporium*. I'm going to prove to Mum that I'm really keen and enthusiastic, and she should let me work there. But when I get there, Mum's not even around. Jolanta is sitting on the high stool by the till, flipping through a tattered copy of *Glamour*. The bell tinkles when I open the door.

Jolanta looks up. 'Oh, it's you,' she says, as I come inside. To me, that seems like a rude way to greet someone. But Mum says that if Jolanta sometimes sounds a little rude, it's because English isn't her first language. I wish Mum would stop apologizing for her.

'Hi, Jolanta,' I say. 'Where's Mum?'

She takes in my outfit – the Fair Isle leggings and the T-shirt (I took off the holey jumper before coming here) – with a smug little smirk. 'At the doctor's – didn't she tell you?'

That's another thing about Jolanta – she's always pretending that Mum lets her in on major secrets that she'd never tell me because I'm a kid. I mean, obviously I *know* she's older. She's eighteen, and has a boyfriend, and is living in a foreign country. But still . . .

I've really tried to like her (no, really, I have!), but I just get this feeling that she wishes that she was Mum's daughter instead of me. The bad thing is, sometimes I think Mum wishes that too.

'Yeah, she did mention it,' I lie. Why is Mum going to the doctor? For a second I forget about Jolanta and worry about Mum. She didn't seem sick to me – or maybe I just didn't notice. 'I just thought she'd be back by now.'

'You can come back later.' Jolanta flicks her hand like she's shooing me away. 'Or I can tell her you came by.'

'Actually, I think I'll stay.' I give her a wicked grin. 'I'm going to be helping out in the shop some afternoons – *didn't she tell you*?'

That gets her attention all right.

'You?' Jolanta frowns.

'Yeah, me.' I keep smiling.

She stands up. 'And I suppose you think I'm going to show you what to do?'

'That's OK,' I say with a shrug. 'If you want to get to work, I could sit there and read your magazine.'

She grabs the magazine and shoves it underneath the counter. 'Eliza told me to mind the till,' she says haughtily. 'But there's some sorting out in the back that needs doing. I'll show you.'

One—nil to her, I think, as I follow her to the back. Minding the till is one thing, but sorting through old clothes gives me goosebumps. The back room of Mum's shop is a cross between a charity shop, a sewing workshop and a tip. There's a little kitchen along one wall with used coffee cups and spoons on the draining board, and a few packets of biscuits that turn out to be just crumbs in a wrapper. Another part of the room is where Mum has her sewing machine and a huge ironing board with a faded rainbow cover and a pile of clothing on top. There are a couple of half-clothed dress forms near the machine, and a pile of random arms, legs and heads of unused mannequins. But well over half of the room is filled with floor-to-ceiling stacks of overflowing bin bags. Most of the bin bags come from house clearances that Mum goes to. (This usually happens when someone dies, or has to go into a home. Their relatives don't want their old things, so Mum clears out all their clothing. It's kind of sad, really.) There are also lots of smaller shopping bags that people leave on the doorstep, like *Eliza's* is some kind of charity shop.

Jolanta points to the ginormous pile. 'You can

learn to do the sorting,' she says.

'Sure,' I say. 'What am I looking for?'

'Make a pile of the good stuff,' she says. 'Anything with a good label – high-street or designer. Or anything that has nice fabric. Or is a classic style.'

I look at her like she's joking. When does anything like that *ever* come into Mum's shop?

'What about the rest of the stuff?' I say.

'Throw it in there.' She points to a huge hospital laundry bin on wheels.

'And what if I don't know?'

'Make another pile.' With a shrug, she goes back through the curtain to the front of the shop.

My skin feels itchy as I pick up one of the smaller bags. A cloud of dust flies up and I sneeze. I hold the bag at arm's length and tear it open. Inside is a pile of old jeans that look like someone wore them for weeks on end without washing them. Underneath are some faded T-shirts, a couple of greyish bras and a few pairs of odd socks with holes in the toes. I don't bother to look at the labels – or the styles or the fabrics. I toss everything in the throwaway bin.

The next bag is even worse. It's full of stinky old shoes – mostly high heels with the little plastic bits rubbed off the heels, and sandals that look like someone found them buried on a beach. There's a pair of boots that are crusted with mud. Somehow, the dried mud gets all over the floor. I'm totally fed up as I throw all of the stuff in the bin.

The next bag doesn't even have clothes in it at all – unless you count some old rags and a dirty blue hoodie. There's also a fossilized sandwich and some empty cans of baked beans and tuna. The bag is so smelly that I take it out the back door and leave it outside on the step. My face is hot with anger. How dare people use Mum's shop like it's a tip? Now that the council only collects the rubbish bins once a fortnight, who knows what might be in the bags? Somebody ought to do something – like check the bags when they come in. Keep the good stuff and make people take the rest of the stuff home to get rid of themselves. That's what I would do if it was up to me.

The bell on the front door tinkles. I stop sorting and listen. A woman has come in looking for a costume for a fifties dance. Jolanta directs her to a rack of dresses. Less than a minute later, the bell tinkles again. The customer has gone. I sigh. So far, working here has been pretty dire.

I scan the bags trying to find one that might have something decent. One of them catches my eye. Unlike the others, it's made of thick white paper with a cord handle. The logo reads: *Galeries Lafayette.* I pull the bag out of the pile.

As soon as I open it, I wonder if there's been some kind of mistake. The clothes inside are folded up neatly, each wrapped in plastic. I take out the first one — a soft blouse made of pale watery blue silk. The fabric is softer than anything I've ever touched before. Handling it carefully, I check the label: it's from Yves St Laurent — which I know is a French designer!

What on earth is it doing here?

I hold the blouse to my nose and breathe in. I imagine where it might have come from — a Paris department store: all spotless black-and-white marble, chrome and glass, racks of beautiful clothes, shoes and handbags everywhere. Just thinking about it makes my knees feel a little weak. I refold the blouse and place it to one side. I take out the next garment from the bag. It's a cropped wool jacket in black-and-white hounds-tooth check, with long sleeves and a wide leather belt. It looks really retro — something you could wear with jeans or a smart skirt. I go through the rest — a black beaded dress, a gold silk skirt, a tailored grey suit — all are designer, and all in perfect condition, like they're brand-new. I can almost imagine the woman who wore these things: tall and slender, but also confident, sure of herself. Walking around Paris in a jaunty beret, maybe with a tiny dog in her handbag. What I can't imagine is why anyone like that would leave these things at Mum's shop.

At the bottom of the bag there's one thing left – I open it carefully like a chocolate wrapped in foil. It's a dress in black silk with a white polka-dot pattern; it has a heart-shaped neckline, cap sleeves, a narrow waist and a full skirt that flares out with layers of sparkly tulle underneath. The label on the dress is Chanel. The fabric is soft and shiny when it catches the light, and the pattern is fun and flirty, and yet elegant at the same time. It might be from the fifties or it might have been made yesterday. A word I've read in fashion magazines pops into my head: 'timeless'.

I look around, almost like someone might be watching me, but of course, I'm alone. Before I can talk myself out of it, I put the dress on over my top and leggings, and do up the hidden zip at the side. It's a perfect fit. All of a sudden, I'm a different girl – a princess, Cinderella going to the ball, a sophisticated Parisian girl – I'm someone I've never wanted, or imagined myself to be, but why not? I stand up a little straighter and parade the length of the room like a catwalk model. The skirt swishes and moves as I walk. There's a mirror on the wall next to the washing machine. Yes, I'm wearing the dress over my old clothes, and my hair is a stringy mess, but I barely even notice. The dress is beautiful and classy . . . I look good.

The front doorbell tinkles again. This time I hear Mum's voice – she's talking to Jolanta. I quickly pull the dress off over my head and shove it back into the bag.

I hear Jolanta telling Mum that I'm here. 'Is she?' I hear her say, sounding surprised. Then there are footsteps coming towards me. All of a sudden, I realize how my heart is racing. I just can't bear the thought of these beautiful things being jammed on a rack with all of the rest of the clothing in Mum's shop. Without a second thought, I take the white bag and shove it back underneath the others.

Mum comes into the stockroom, hands on hips. 'Andy,' she says, her lips pursed. 'What are you doing?'

'I'm sorting through stock.'

'I can see that.'

'Jolanta told me to.'

'I thought we agreed that you're too young to work here. You need to be focusing on school. If you study hard and do well in your GCSEs, then you might be able to go to uni some day. It's really important.'

'You said you'd think about it.'

She sighs. I take a good look at her. Her face looks kind of pasty, and I notice that there are strands of white in her long brown hair. She walks over to one of the dress forms. There's a shapeless lilac cardigan on it with tacky gold buttons hanging half off. I watch as she gets a pair of scissors and snips the buttons off one by one. Then she takes out a plastic tray that's filled with all kinds of funky buttons in different colours.

'The thing is,' she says, picking up a needle and thread. 'I can't pay you.'

I watch as she begins sewing different coloured buttons on to the purple cardigan – red, green, yellow, sky blue. I know it should be job done, conversation over: if Mum won't pay me then there's no reason to stay. I glance at the pile of bin bags where I've hidden my find. Now that I'm here, I feel reluctant to leave.

Mum finishes sewing the buttons. When she's finished she holds it up. 'Good as new,' she says breezily.

'It's nice, Mum.' I have to admit, the quirky buttons do look a lot better than the hideous gold ones.

'You can have it if you want.' She holds it out to me. 'Consider it payment for the work you've done today.'

I shrink back. The new buttons may look good, but it's still a shapeless lilac cardigan. 'Um, it's not really my style,' I say, hoping I don't hurt her feelings too much.

'OK.' She shrugs. 'Well, I think it's cute.' She looks at the label. 'And it came from the Edinburgh Woollen Mill.'

Which to me explains the ugly buttons.

She shakes it out. 'I'll put it on Amelie,' she says.

'Who?'

'She's the mannequin by the till.'

'Oh.' I try not to dwell on the fact that Mum has names for her mannequins.

She starts to walk off.

'Maybe I could choose something else,' I say.

'What's that?' She stops.

'As payment. I'm sure I could find something else that I like.'

'Fine, Andy,' she says.

She goes through the curtain to dress 'Amelie', leaving me there. As soon as she's gone, I dig the nice bag out of the pile. I take out all the clothing and put it into a spare bin liner – everything but the polka-dot dress. I bury the bin liner at the bottom of the stack – Mum and Jolanta can discover it on their own, like treasure buried beneath a mound of rubbish. I put the polka-dot dress back into the white bag and try to fold the bag up and put it in my rucksack. It's too big, so I find another bin liner and put it inside. Finally, I grab a pair of nasty old jeans out of the throwaway bin.

Mum and Jolanta are talking in quiet voices at the till as I come up to them carrying my rucksack and the bin bag. 'I'll take these jeans, if that's OK?' I hold them up. 'And I probably ought to go home now to do my homework.'

Jolanta looks down at the black plastic bin liner.

'I've also got to wash my gym kit.' I wave my hand in front of my face. 'Phew, it stinks.'

'You can leave it here if you like,' Mum says. 'I'll be doing some laundry later.'

'No, that's OK,' I say, feeling frazzled. 'It . . . um, isn't that dirty.'

Jolanta raises an eyebrow. I wonder if she's on to me. I leave the shop carrying the bag. *I'm not doing anything wrong*, I say to myself.

So why do I feel so guilty?

6

OPERATION NEW CLOTHES

Technically, I haven't done anything wrong. (OK – it was a little bit wrong to lie about the jeans as payment and the bin liner that didn't have my gym clothes. But I get my comeuppance for that when Mum comes home from the shop with a whole bag of tatty old jeans like the pair I took, and I have to pretend to like them.) Mum did say I could take something from the shop as payment, so I took the polka-dot dress. I haven't broken any laws, or disobeyed any of the Ten Commandments or anything like that. If I had to stand before St Peter at the pearly gates and explain why I took the dress, I'd be able to look him in the eye and do it, easy. I just don't feel so keen on explaining it to Mum.

At home, I run upstairs to my room and put the white bag in my wardrobe. It stays there all evening while I do my homework and eat dinner. When Mum comes home, we sit on the sofa and watch a recording of *The Great British Sewing Bee*, and finally head upstairs for bed.

I wait in my room until I hear Mum's bedroom door close and the sound of the bath running. Then I take the white bag out of my wardrobe and pull out the dress. I put it on over my T-shirt and PJ bottoms and parade up and down my room, catching a glimpse of a me I don't recognize in the mirror on the back of the door. A me that maybe I can be some day when I'm grown up. But not yet. I take off the polka-dot dress. There's a part of me — a big part, actually — that regrets what I've decided to do.

As soon as I'm sure Mum's in the bath, I sneak downstairs with the dress to Mum's workroom just off the kitchen. She's got a sewing machine and a full-sized dress form at home that she uses for doing alterations. I move the form in front of the plain white wall and put the polka-dot dress on it, arranging the layers of tulle so that the skirt puffs out. Then, using an old digital camera I got for Christmas a few years ago, I snap a bunch of pictures of the dress from different angles. I take it off the mannequin and photograph the label, making sure that the 'Chanel' is perfectly clear.

I'm just about finished when the phone rings, making me jump half out of my skin. For a second, I worry that someone's found me out – they're calling to blackmail me – threatening to go to the police . . .

The message machine clicks on. It's Aunt Linda – Mum's sister – calling for a chat. She lives up in the Lake District where Mum's from, and even though it's far away, they're still pretty close. Halfway through the message, I can hear Mum's voice – she's picked up from the extension in her room.

My hands are shaking as I quickly shove the dress form back in the corner, fold up the polka-dot dress and put it back in the bag. I sneak back upstairs to my room and return the bag to the wardrobe. I jump into bed and pull the duvet over my head.

Step One complete.

The next day, it's time for Step Two. I log on to eBay from the computer in the school library. It isn't hard to open an account under my name. When it flashes on the screen for me to confirm that I've read the terms and conditions and that I'm over eighteen, I take a deep breath and click 'yes'. It's that easy. I click on 'sell an item' and I'm good to go.

A screen comes up with lots of little blanks for me to fill in. The first thing is the listing description. I start with 'Vintage Chanel black-and-white dress' and hit enter. But that sounds so bland. I go back and change it to 'Beautiful One-of-a-Kind Polka-Dot Dress by Chanel' which sounds a little better. Next I fill in the other details prompted by the screen. Last of all, there's a blank for 'price' – the most important thing. I have absolutely no idea what to put in. There's a choice between an auction and a 'Buy it Now' – and a little bubble recommending that if you don't know what an item is worth, do an auction. I click 'auction'. Then I have to set a starting price. Another little bubble that says starting the auction at 99p will attract more buyers. Just to be cheeky – and because I have nothing to lose – I put in £100. An absolute fortune! Then, with a sigh, I backspace and put in 99p as the auction starting price.

When I've filled in all the blanks, I upload the photos I took from my camera. Finally, I press 'list'. It takes a few seconds for the little bar to leave the screen, and for a second I wonder if the computer has somehow sussed out that I'm not only underage, but also selling something I shouldn't be. Then the screen flashes 'done'. I press 'view listing'. And there it is – the polka-dot dress, up on the screen among the other dresses. I've done it!

I scroll down and spend some time looking at the other dresses for sale. There are so many listings, and most of them have a starting price of higher than 99p. My heart sinks – I should have aimed higher. I'm about to amend my listing when I see at the bottom of the page that the polka-dot dress has already got one bid – of 99p.

The bell rings and I shut down the computer. I walk off to class feeling a mixture of guilt, disappointment and hope. Am I on my way to a shopping spree – buying bags and bags full of lovely new clothes from all the trendy shops – or on the way to disaster? For now, at least, it's out of my hands.

7

HIDING IN PLAIN SIGHT

After school I go to *Eliza's Emporium* like nothing's happened. I want to convince Mum that I'm serious about having a job (and if I can find any more 'hidden gems' in the back, then that's OK too). It's pouring with rain, and for once I'm almost glad to go inside the shop, where at least it's dry. The bell tinkles as I enter. This time Mum is there. She's wearing a long brown dress with some kind of gold chain print on it. It might have been decent once, but now it's bobbled and faded. It's the kind of thing someone would donate to a charity shop – or *Eliza's Emporium*. Normally Mum looks good in her vintage 'finds', but right now her standards seem to have slipped.

I quickly scan her face to see if she looks OK. I totally forgot that she had a doctor's appointment yesterday, and now I feel bad that I didn't ask about it.

'Oh hi, Andy.' Her smile seems a little forced. 'I wasn't expecting you. I assumed you'd be going over to Stevie's house.'

'I might go later,' I say. 'But seeing as Jolanta's got college today, I thought you could use a hand.'

Mum's face clouds over. 'It's nice that you want to help out, Andy. But really, it's not necessary. I've managed just fine for a long time.'

'Why were you at the doctor's yesterday?' I blurt out. 'You told Jolanta you were going, but not me.'

She looks surprised for a second. Then she begins to laugh. But her eyes don't seem to get the joke. They look red-rimmed and hollow. 'Oh, darling.' She holds out her arms. Like a little kid, I go to her and let her enfold me in a hug. I breathe in the scent of sandalwood and rose, and feel comforted by her warmth. 'You were worried about me, is that it?'

'Yeah, I was.' I rest my head against her shoulder.

'Well, don't worry. I'm going to be fine.'

Going to be. Not *am* fine. I look up at her face. Mum looks . . . old. I know I should ask her to tell me more, but honestly, I feel scared. All I want is for her to be back the way she was before.

She lets me go. Like she's read my thoughts, she gives me a broad smile – the way she used to. 'So it's OK if you want to go,' she says. 'Or you can stay and keep me company.'

'Um, I guess I'll stay for a while.' I smile back, even though I'm still worried about her. 'I may go over to Stevie's later to finish my homework.'

'Sounds like a plan,' Mum says. 'Now, since you're here, I need to do a couple of things in the back. Do you think you can watch the till?'

'OK. Yeah,' I say eagerly. If she's trusting me to watch the till, she must be coming round to my being here.

'Just shout if you need help.'

'I will.' I watch as she picks up a pile of clothing and squeezes through the maze of racks. The shop is way too small for all the stuff that's in it. If it were mine, I'd get rid of half of the clothes on the racks so that customers could actually see what's there. Then I'd sort things by colour, or maybe just stick to a few seasonal colours. I don't know.

Mum pauses by a rack of baby clothes and straightens a giraffe onesie that's half off its hanger. I can see from here that it's greyish and faded. I can't believe anyone would buy something that someone else's baby has pooped and vomited in. If it were up to me, I'd definitely get rid of the baby clothes. Next to the baby clothes are the tartan dog coats. Mum's accessorized them with matching bows. Even though they've been washed, there are still some strands of reddish dog hair on them. Maybe it's a good thing that customers *can't* see what's here.

I turn away and stare out the window. Rain is dripping from the awning in front of the shop. It's ripped in a couple of places, and there's greenish black mould growing underneath. I'd get rid of that too.

I straighten a few things next to the till – a stapler, the pile of business cards (I pick one up and look at it – I'd definitely get rid of that 'New to U!' logo), and I refold the carbon paper in the receipt book so that it's ready to write up the next sale. Out of interest, I flip through the ones on top that have been folded back. A hole slowly begins to form in my stomach. Yesterday, the takings for *Eliza's Emporium* amounted to £18. And in the week before, the total came to £89. Compared to some of the prices I saw on eBay for a single item, that seems like a tiny amount for a whole shop.

I close the receipt book. The shop suddenly seems very cold. No wonder Mum says she can't pay me. She's making practically nothing! I'm not sure why I'm surprised, but I *am* surprised. Mum's had her shop for a long time. She always talks like she has loads of customers and makes, if not lots of money, at least enough to get by. I also know that there are lots of people out there who are into vintage. The shop *should* be making money, not losing it. No wonder she hasn't seemed herself lately. She must be really worried. I just wish she'd told me.

The bell on the front door tinkles. An elderly woman wearing a navy raincoat and yellow welly boots comes in, dragging with her a small, muddy black-and-white dog on a leash. The dog shakes its wet fur all over the floor – and a rack of blouses. 'Sit, Henry,' the woman says.

'Hello,' I say, standing up. Surely Mum must have heard the bell. But she hasn't come out of the stockroom and I can hear the dryer going full tilt – maybe she didn't hear. If the woman notices that I'm only thirteen and not officially working here, she doesn't let on.

'How much is that cardigan in the window?' she says.

I look at the mannequin where she's pointing – 'Amelie'. It's the lilac cardigan that Mum sewed the colourful buttons on to. I check the sleeve where Mum usually puts the tags. There's one pinned to the arm that says £3. In an instant, the truth flashes before my eyes. No wonder the shop is losing so much money!

Right then and there, I decide not to get Mum. 'It's thirteen pounds,' I say, thinking quickly. 'Would you like to try it on?'

'Thirteen pounds?' The woman looks horrified. 'I've never paid more than a fiver for anything at this shop.'

I take the cardigan off the mannequin. 'This cardigan is very high quality,' I say. 'It's made from pure wool. And the buttons have been sewed on specially by hand. It's a one-of-a-kind piece.' I hold it out to her so that she can feel the material. 'It's soft and warm, and it will last for years.'

'Well . . .' She runs her fingers over the knit and checks the buttons.

'You really have to try it on,' I say. 'I'm sure it will be perfect for you. I mean, you need to be wearing something warm when you're out walking the dog. Um . . . Henry.'

The woman looks a little startled, but she removes her raincoat. I hand her the cardigan and help her into it, making sure she does up all the buttons. I'm relieved that it fits her, and even looks kind of good in an old-lady-walking-the-dog-in-the-rain kind of way.

'The length is very flattering on you,' I say. 'And the colour looks good too.'

There's a mirror by the till with some old beads and scarves draped over it. I sweep them to the side so that she can see for herself.

'Um, it is nice . . .' She turns and looks at herself from all angles. I can see, though, that she's still a little hesitant.

'Tell you what,' I say. 'I can do a special rainy day discount just for you. Ten pounds.'

'Ten pounds.' She looks at the dog. 'What do you think, Henry?'

The dog barks sharply, making me jump.

'OK, I think I have it.' She digs in the pocket of her coat and pulls out a roll of notes – mostly twenties. She peels off two shiny fivers and hands them to me.

'Thank you,' I say. 'Would you like to wear it or should I wrap it up?'

'I'll wear it.'

'OK.' I feel fizzy with adrenalin at having made the sale. I remove the £3 tag and toss it in the bin. Then I help her back into her raincoat.

'Are you new here?' the woman says. 'You seem a little young.'

'I'm Eliza's daughter. I'll be helping out—'

Just then, Mum rushes in from the back.

'I thought I heard voices,' she says. 'Oh, hello, Mrs Whiting. Hello, Henry.' She bends down to pet the wet dog.

The woman purses her lips as she looks at Mum. 'Your daughter is quite the salesgirl, Eliza,' she says. 'You could learn a thing or two from her.' She tugs Henry's leash and pulls him back out of the shop into the rain. She gives us both a little wave as the door shuts behind them.

'What did she mean by that?' Mum says.

I write up the sale in the receipt book. 'Ten pounds,' I say. 'Another ten and you'll be doing better than yesterday.'

Mum puts her hands on her hips. 'Ten pounds for that cardigan?'

'Yeah, I gave her a discount.' I shrug. 'The tag said thirteen. Hope that's OK?'

I look her in the eye, daring her to call my bluff. She opens her mouth, then closes it again.

'Of course,' she says, swallowing hard. 'I don't mind knocking off a pound or two here and there to make a sale.'

8

A THIEF IN THE NIGHT

After my amazing sale, I'm eager to stay and see if I can make another. But soon two more customers come in who know Mum and are clearly there to 'talk vintage'. I try to listen in and learn something, but I feel frustrated when one of them leaves without buying anything, and the other buys a leopard-print belt for £3.99. I want to talk to Mum about the shop and the prices, and why people aren't buying more stuff. But before I can do so, she bustles off to the back to find another belt to restock the rack. I'm on my own when the bell tinkles and the door opens again.

'Oh!' I put my hand to my mouth when a tall

woman with reddish-brown hair walks in. She's wearing a tight black skirt, knee-high black boots and a bright red silk blouse. 'Ms Cartwright,' I say. 'It's um . . .'

Really weird, I want to say. Ms Cartwright is a teacher at my school, and I have her for 'Learning about the World'. She used to be *Mr* Cartwright, but then she went through three years of gender reassignment. At first, kids talked and laughed about it, which was really just mean and pointless. But she was totally open and upfront about it, and personally I think she's pretty brave. Now, most people just accept it. I guess that's what we 'learned about the world' from her – if something isn't a secret, it loses its shock value. Still, I'm a little shocked to see her here. I've always thought she dressed quite smartly compared to the other teachers. I didn't have her down as someone who shopped at *Eliza's Emporium*.

'. . . nice to see you,' I finish.

'Hi, Andy.' She smiles like she's glad to see me, and not at all embarrassed. 'I haven't seen you here before.'

'It's my mum's shop,' I say. 'I'm getting some work experience.'

'Good for you.' She lowers her voice conspiratorially. 'Maybe I can get you to keep an eye out for anything new and fabulous that comes in. Give me a tip-off?'

'Sure,' I say, smiling back. I think immediately about the clothes in the back that I shoved underneath the other bin bags. They're probably way too small to fit Ms Cartwright, but if Mum wasn't here, I might show them to her.

'Georgia.' Mum sweeps up to us, her bracelets clanking. 'Lovely to see you.' She puts a hand on Ms Cartwright's arm.

'Yes, I was just having a nice chat with Andy,' she says to Mum. 'But really, I've come to look at the shoes—' She breaks off and goes over to another rack. 'This is pretty, isn't it?'

My face goes as red as the lacy bra she's holding up. 'I'll um . . . leave you to it,' I say, though I don't think either of them hears me. Mum seems fine, and I really do have homework to do. And, OK, I'm really not keen on being here while Ms Cartwright tries on shoes . . . or anything else.

I go over to Stevie's house just in time for dinner. Her mum helped her and Carrie make a big pot of spaghetti with meatballs and tomato sauce for us to eat and now I can hear her talking on the phone to someone in another room. I tell them all about my new job – about how I made a sale, and about Ms Cartwright coming in to look for shoes. (I keep the part about the bra to myself. I also haven't told them about taking the polka-dot dress and listing it on eBay.)

'Ha!' Stevie says. 'I'm *so* not surprised that Ms Cartwright's a regular at the *Emporium.*'

'Really?' I say. 'I think she usually looks good.'

'I guess she knows how to find those hidden gems,' Carrie says.

'Yeah, maybe. It's just . . .' Suddenly my eyes fill with tears.

'What's the matter?' Stevie says. 'It sounds like it wasn't as bad as you thought.'

'It's not that.' I wipe away a tear and tell them about how I looked in the receipt book and added up the numbers. How Mum's shop is losing money and I wish there was something I could do about it.

Stevie wheels up and puts her hand on my arm. 'It's OK, Andy. Look – it's early days. You've got some good ideas that might really help. Like raising the prices and giving the place a good clear-out.'

'But Mum won't listen to me! She doesn't even want me there. She wants to have long chats about vintage clothing with Jolanta and her regular customers who come in and either don't buy anything, or else grab what they can for a fiver.'

'Have you tried to talk to her?' Stevie says.

'No. But what's the point? It's her shop. She doesn't see it the same way I do.'

'I don't know,' Carrie says. 'You've been talking for five whole minutes without whingeing about the smell – maybe you're getting used to the place.'

'Great.' I shake my head.

Stevie sets the table as Carrie and I bring the pasta over. 'So what's up with you two?' I say. When I first got here, they both seemed a little quiet. And even though we'd hung out earlier at school, spending time in Mum's shop has made it feel like a lot longer.

Stevie and Carrie exchange a look. All of a sudden, I realize that the whole conversation up until now has been about me.

'What?' I say warily.

'We've got some news too,' Stevie says.

'OK . . .'

'Actually, mine is good news,' she says. 'I'm going to that place in Cambridgeshire that I mentioned. They're going to teach my legs how to walk.'

'That's so fab!' I bend over and give her a hug.

'Just think – you'll be out of the chair!'

'Yeah. It is.' For some reason, Stevie doesn't seem as excited as I'd have thought. 'So anyway, I won't be around after school on Fridays from now on. And we're going for an introductory session tomorrow evening too.'

'It's really brilliant,' I say. I go to the stove where Carrie's serving up the meatballs. They smell delicious. I pick one up and pop it into my mouth. 'Yum,' I say. 'You want one?' I go to reach for another.

'No thanks.' Carrie shakes her head. 'In fact, I think I'm going to have a yogurt instead of pasta.'

'Yogurt?' I say, frowning. 'Why?'

She stares down at the meatballs, her mouth set in a straight line. 'My news isn't good,' she says. 'Dad has signed me up for some boot camp thing at the weekend. I have to start going there every weekend and even staying over on Saturday nights.'

'Boot camp?' I say. 'Sounds scary. What do you have to do there?'

'Dieting and exercise.' She winces.

'But why? I mean, you're fine the way you are.'

'Thanks. But not everyone thinks that. Dad says it's not about losing weight – though it is, obviously – but about being healthy and getting fit. He's doing it with me on the Sunday. I guess he thinks we need some more bonding time and all that.'

'Oh.' I can't work out whether it's a good or bad thing. Carrie and her dad are on their own, like me and Mum. Her parents are divorced and her mum lives up north somewhere. 'I guess bonding time sounds good.'

'Yeah. I just wish we could bond at the cinema or at the mall. Maybe take a cookery course. You know – something fun?'

'Did you tell him that?'

'No – but what's the point? He's already signed us up.' She shrugs her shoulders, looking glum.

'Well, I guess you'll just have to see how it goes,' I say.

'Sounds like we all need a dose of good luck,' Stevie says.

'Yeah,' I say. 'We do.'

We eat dinner, clear up and then do our homework. Afterwards, I ask Stevie if I can use her iPad for a minute. She wheels it over and I open up eBay. When I log into my seller dashboard, I practically fall over backwards. The polka-dot dress already has twenty-three watchers, six bids, and is at £106.60! And the auction still has two whole days to go. I feel mega amazing and mega guilty all at the same time. But one thing I'm sure about is that if it was for sale in Mum's shop, it wouldn't be selling for anywhere near a hundred pounds. It was wrong of me to take the dress without showing it to Mum first. But I can always give back the money to help the shop. Or some of it . . . maybe . . .

I close down the site before my friends can ask me what I'm looking at. Then I gather my things to go home.

Outside, the night is dark and clear. It takes me about five minutes to walk to the high street. The pub at one end is still open, and when I pass the chippie I see Mr LeBoeff inside mopping the floor. I wave to him, but his lips are puckered like he's whistling, and he doesn't see me. Next door is the old theatre. I pause briefly but I don't see any lights inside or hear any music. Did I imagine it?

I pass Mum's shop. With the lilac cardigan sold, 'Amelie' is now wearing a black dress that actually looks good – I mean, it's hard to ruin a black dress – with several long strings of pearls around the neck. I step back from the window, trying to imagine what the window might be like if all the mannequins had little black dresses on and the wedding display was taken down, when all of a sudden I see a light flickering in the back of the shop. I freeze, my heart in my throat. The light flickers again – it's a torch. Someone is inside!

It's just not fair! Anger surges in my chest. Mum barely makes any money from the shop, and now someone is trying to rob her. I'm not going to let that happen! I race around the side of the shop to the alley behind. Maybe I should try to contact the police, but I don't have a phone so I can't call them. All I can do is try to scare off the intruder.

The back door to the shop is wide open. My whole body is in a cold sweat as I tiptoe closer and look inside. I see the torch – its beam is propped up on Mum's ironing board. Someone is rifling through the mountain of plastic bags. It might be a good thing if a burglar took all the stuff, but what if they've already taken the cash? My cheeks burn with anger. I made Mum ten pounds, and it had better *not* be stolen.

'Who's there?' I call out in a loud forceful voice.

The rustling stops. It's like the intruder is hoping that if they keep still, I'll just go away. But I'm not going anywhere. My hand is shaking as I reach up beside the door and flip on the light switch.

The overhead lights flicker for a second, and then go on full force. And I'm face to face with the burglar!

9

THE OLD THEATRE

'Oh, it's you!' I blurt out at the same time he says, 'Andrea?'

I'm ashamed to say that a whole lot of my anger just melts away when I see those blue-grey eyes.

'Thomas,' I say, trying to pronounce it like his uncle did. 'What are you doing here?'

He stands up from where he's been crouching down over the pile of bags. 'I can explain,' he says.

'Yeah, you'd better.' I put my hands on my hips.

He goes over to the ironing board and turns off the torch. 'Good, now I can save the batteries.' He gives me a broad smile.

'Well?' I say, refusing to be charmed.

'For one thing, Andy, your mum shouldn't leave a key to the shop under the mat at the back. I mean, you're just asking for trouble.'

'And I guess you found it. Even with a key it's still breaking and entering.'

He frowns. 'If I was a thief, don't you think I'd break into the betting shop or something? No offence, but I don't think your mum has much here that I'd like to steal.'

'Oh yeah?' I *am* a little offended. 'Then what are you doing here?'

'Looking for something that belongs to me,' he says. 'A big white bag with a black handle. It says *Galeries Lafayette* on it.'

The breath freezes in my lungs. 'Why do you think it's here?' I say.

'Because the dry-cleaner messed up. They were supposed to return it to the chippie, but instead they left it on the wrong doorstep. No one was here when I got off work, so I just thought I'd come in and have a look. Take it back before anyone noticed.'

'Dry-cleaning?' I say, unable to hide my surprise.

His eyes narrow, and for a second I think he's on to me. 'Yeah,' he says. 'I thought they were doing me a favour when they said they'd drop it by. But now it's gone.'

I rewind back to my Really Bad Decision – taking the polka-dot dress and hiding the rest of the designer stuff in the stack of bin bags. Mum hasn't mentioned any great new stock so I'm pretty sure it must still be there. But if I tell him that or accidentally 'find' the bag I buried, then I'll have to come clean about the dress too.

'What was in the bag?' I say, covering my tracks. 'Maybe Mum's been through it if it was here.'

'It was designer clothing that belonged to my aunt. It's very valuable. There was a wool jacket by Moschino, a Chanel dress and some other things. All designer originals.'

'Your aunt?' Feeling dizzy, I sit down on Mum's sewing stool. What have I done?

'Yeah. It was totally stupid of me to trust someone else with it. I see that now. I really don't want my uncle to find out.'

His uncle . . . this is getting worse and worse.

'Hey, don't worry, OK.' I smile. 'Maybe it will turn up. I'm helping out at the shop now, so I can have a look tomorrow after school.' I sweep my hand around the room. 'I mean, it *might* be here somewhere.'

'OK, thanks.' He starts to walk to the door. I should just let him go. It's safest for me that way.

But I'm curious about the clothing – and about him.

'Do you want a Coke or something?' I say. 'Mum has a fridge.' I point to the little fridge that's under one of the work tables.

He leans against the wall. 'Is this how you treat all of your burglars?'

'Not all of them.' *Only the really gorgeous ones.* I go to the fridge and take out two Cokes. I throw one to him and he catches it. 'Was that you in the old theatre the other night?' I ask. 'Did they leave a key under the mat there too?'

He stares at me. 'What? How did you know—?'

'You just told me,' I say triumphantly. 'But really, I saw the light through the boards and I heard music.'

'Are you often out late at night?'

'I usually do my homework at a friend's house. I walk by here on my way home.'

'Well, that explains it,' he says. 'But I didn't think anyone could see the light.'

'What were you doing there?'

He drinks his Coke down in a single swig. 'It's a long story,' he says.

I cross my arms. 'I've got time.'

'A picture's worth a thousand words. You want to come and see?'

'Yeah, sure.' My heart speeds up at the thought of going anywhere with him.

'But you need to keep it a secret, OK?'

'Fine. That's two you owe me.' I blush, thinking of the secret I'm already keeping – from him.

He gives me a sideways glance. 'I guess so.'

We throw our Coke cans in the recycling and leave Mum's shop. He puts the key back under the mat – it *is* a pretty rubbish place to hide a key. Then he takes out another key and we go to the building next door.

'Your mum's shop used to be part of the theatre,' he says, unlocking the door. 'I think it was the old café.'

'Really?' I wonder if Mum knows.

'It was split off as a separate shop sometime before my uncle bought the theatre.' He puts the key back in his pocket.

'Mr LeBoeff owns the theatre?'

'Yeah. He bought it when he moved here from Paris. I was only like three or something. It was before my aunt – his wife – died. A long time ago.'

He flicks a switch and a dim light comes on. I follow him inside the door into a corridor.

'This was the stage door,' he says, closing it behind us. 'There are a few dressing rooms back here.' He gestures to the closed doors that we walk past. At the end of the corridor are some steps at the side leading to the stage. I follow him through a thick velvet curtain that leads to the main theatre. He flicks another switch, and all of a sudden everything is flooded with light.

'Oh!' I stop and stare, my mouth wide open.

I don't know what I was expecting – some kind of pokey old cinema with moth-eaten red velvet seats, a floor sticky with chewing gum and stuck-on sweets. Instead, we're standing in a huge room that's completely empty and completely white – or kind of a dingy yellowish colour – except for a fancy wood floor in a zigzag pattern. The walls are plaster with garlands of flowers and fruit at the top. There are columns down the side of the room with fancy tops. A ladder has been propped up by the wall next to the stage, and underneath is a spattered plastic cloth. The room smells of fresh paint and the wall that Thomas has been painting is a bright, clean white.

'It's amazing,' I say. 'I had no idea this was here. I thought it was an old cinema.'

'It used to be a social club and dance hall,' Thomas says. 'During the war, they had huge dances here for the RAF soldiers. And there's a rumour that The Beatles played here when they were first starting out.'

'The Beatles? Really?' I wonder if Stevie knows. She loves old music like that.

'Yeah.' He walks over to one of the columns and picks at a fleck of chipped paint. 'Then for a while there was an old lady who gave dance lessons here. When she died, the place was boarded up.'

'I just can't believe it's here, right on the other side of the wall from Mum's shop.'

'It's a good space,' he says. 'And it'll look a lot better once I paint it. It'll take me a couple of weeks – it's so huge.'

'And then what?' I say. 'What are you going to do with it?'

Thomas shrugs. 'I'm hoping my uncle will sell it. There's no reason to keep it.' His face suddenly clouds over. 'Coming here was a mistake. I mean, my uncle used to be a chef in Paris. He had his own café and everything. And look at him now.'

'A chef?' I can't really imagine Mr LeBoeff as anything other than the man who sells fish and chips on the high street. Though his fish and chips are pretty amazing.

'I'm serious.' Thomas seems to sense my disbelief.

'Then why *did* he come here?'

'Because of my aunt,' he says. 'She was a famous

fashion model in Paris. She knew all the great designers — like Yves St Laurent, Gianni Versace, Oscar de la Renta. But then she got cancer. Her sister lived near here, so they moved here to be closer to family.'

'Oh.' I struggle to take this all in. Mum and Mr LeBoeff have been shop neighbours for a long time, but I didn't know any of this. I guess I never thought to ask.

'My uncle thought she was going to get better. He's really positive like that. My aunt saw the old theatre and fell in love with it, so my uncle bought it for her. They were going to do something with it, but then she died. I guess he's kept it all these years because he's sentimental. But I really think he needs to move on. He's talked before about wanting to go back to Paris. He still has friends there, and family. I know he'd be much happier.'

'So you're fixing it up to sell?' What Thomas is saying makes sense, but for some reason I feel a little disappointed.

'Yeah,' he says. 'When I've got it looking up to scratch, I'll get an estate agent round to value it. Then I'll tell my uncle.'

'What?' I stare at him in surprise. 'You haven't told him what you're planning?'

'No.' He stares at the floor. 'Like I said, he's sentimental. But if I get everything arranged, then he'll see that it's for the best.'

'OK . . .?'

'But in the meantime, I'd appreciate it if you kept it quiet. I don't want him to find out what I'm doing.'

I make a motion to zip my lips. 'Your secret's safe with me.'

10

ANGELS AND DEVILS

L ater on, when I finally get to bed (after another telling-off from Mum for being home so late), I can't sleep. My mind keeps turning over and over – I just can't believe that all this time, right next door to Mum's shop, there's this amazing place – the old theatre. If it belonged to me, there's no way I would sell it. But I understand why Thomas would want to do so.

Thomas . . . Before tonight, he's always seemed a little scary. But now that we've actually talked and I've learned something about his family, I see that he's fine. If only I could tell my friends – they would be so jealous. But I said I would keep it quiet, and besides, he's probably going to hate me once he figures out that I took the polka-dot dress and hid the rest of the clothing. I should have just confessed that I found it – the dry-cleaner obviously left it on the wrong doorstep. Why didn't I? Now I've taken something from not just one person but two – three, if you count the dead aunt who was a fashion model in Paris.

I go to school early and head straight to the library. I'm going to stop the auction – it's the right thing to do. I open the listing for the polka-dot dress and practically fall over. It's up to £325! I hover over the button that says 'end auction'. I should give the dress back to Thomas. But then I wouldn't be able to give any of the money back to Mum. And what about the forty-three people who have all placed bids? Surely I owe it to them to see it through? I could still give the money back to Thomas – or we could split it three ways.

Or – I could stick to my original plan. Keep the money and buy a whole new wardrobe at my favourite shops. As long as I change my clothes at school, Mum need never know. I feel like there's an angel and a devil perched on opposite shoulders. They're both shouting in my ears and doing my head in.

On my way to class, I duck into the girls' loos and check my reflection in the mirror. I hate everything about my outfit – all of it from Mum's shop. Baggy jeans, a tie-dye top, a navy cardigan with big pockets and a pair of 'pre-loved' Converse high tops. Who wore these things before me? Someone fab – or someone horrible?

One of the cubicle doors bangs and Chloe walks out. *The fashion police!* I've been caught red-handed.

'Hi, Andy,' she says, eyeing my outfit.

'Hi.' I stare back at her, and realize that she's wearing *the skirt* – the brown corduroy one with the patchwork spots from Asos that looked so cute online. She's accessorized it with a mint-green top, a studded denim jacket, brown tights and slouchy suede boots with a little heel. The skin on the back of my neck begins to itch with envy.

'I like your shoes,' she says. 'Converse are cool.'

I stare at her, waiting for her to start laughing – like I'd actually believe she might pay me a compliment. She washes her hands at the sink and puts on lip gloss. When she doesn't laugh, or say anything else, I decide to take a risk.

'I like your skirt,' I say. 'From Asos, right?'

'It was on sale,' she says. 'Only nineteen pounds.'

'Cool.'

She raises an eyebrow and leaves the loos. I

exhale in relief. I've survived. I check my reflection again and take off the cardigan. The thing is, I've seen a few girls in Chloe's crowd wearing similar jeans and the top actually isn't that bad either. I also think about Ms Cartwright. She doesn't seem bothered by the fact that whatever she buys at Mum's shop isn't new. Does it really matter so much? I swallow hard. To me, it does.

At lunchtime, Stevie wheels up to me in the canteen. 'You OK, Andy?' she says. 'You look tired.'

'I had a bit of a late night,' I say. 'I couldn't sleep, so I stayed up reading.'

'Oh? Anything good?'

'Um, I don't know. I fell asleep.'

She peers at me like I'm not going to get off that easily. I wish I could tell her about Thomas but I know it's best not to. Especially since he's bound to hate me if he finds out about the really bad thing I'm doing—

'Remember, I'm not around after school. I'm going for my introductory walking lesson.'

'Brilliant!' I say, hiding the fact that I had forgotten it was today. 'You must be so excited.'

She looks down at her hands folded in her lap. 'Yeah,' she says quietly. I'm startled to see tears in her eyes.

'Stevie, what's wrong?' I put my hand on her shoulder but she pulls away.

'I'm scared,' she says. 'It's going to hurt – a lot. What if it hurts too much? What if I can't do it? It's one thing having no hope of ever walking again – or just wishing that some day I might be able to try. But actually doing it . . . I don't know . . .'

'Hey!' I kneel down and take her hand. 'You will be able to do it. I just know it. You're the smartest and bravest person I've ever met.'

'Smart and brave don't control leg muscles.'

'No, but they control up here.' I tap the side of my head. 'That's got to be a lot of it.'

'Maybe you're the one who's smart, Andy.'

'Me – no way.'

'Well, you seem to know the right thing to say.' She smiles and I smile back, glad to have helped a little.

I stand up again. 'Carrie and I will be wishing you luck. Mind to mind. Like telekinesis.'

'OK,' she says. 'Beam me your energies at exactly half four this afternoon.'

11

THE DARK SIDE

In the late afternoon, I think of Stevie as promised. It would be so great if she could walk again, and I really hope that it all goes well. But by five o'clock, all I can think about is the fact that my auction is ending – I haven't stopped it. I hang around the library and log in for the last seconds. The polka-dot dress sells for a whopping £485! I feel like a balloon has inflated in my stomach and I'm about to float off somewhere – probably to the nearest Westfield shopping centre. It would be brilliant – the best day of my life – if I could go shopping with £485 in my pocket. I could buy bags and bags of the nicest clothes from the sales and the new season. I could spend days just browsing and choosing: Topshop, Next, Zara, Gap, Debenhams. And the shoes; and the handbags, jewellery and hair slides . . . Everything would be brand-new, unworn – nothing 'pre-owned', or 'pre-loved'. I feel like standing up, dancing around, flinging out my arms and giving a great big whoop.

But it's never going to happen.

I click on the 'send invoice to buyer', and close down the website. What I did was wrong. I took the polka-dot dress without clearing it with Mum. The dress belongs to Thomas or his uncle. I sold it on without telling anyone. I don't know for sure, but it sounds like there's at least a few crimes in that.

As I walk home from school, I picture how awful it would be if I was working at Mum's shop when the police came to arrest me. Mum will try to reason with the officers – offer them a cup of tea and a crumby biscuit – 'let's just all sit down and sort this out'. Jolanta will look smug as the policemen say 'no thank you' to the tea and ask me to hold out my wrists so they can cuff them. And when I'm dragged out of the shop to the waiting police car, Mr LeBoeff will stand in the doorway of the chippie looking shocked and disappointed. Worst of all, Thomas will come out of the back where he's been frying chips and washing dishes, and he'll *know* what I've done, and how I lied to him.

Except it doesn't have to be that way.

I can stop all this right now. Give the bag back to Thomas with all the clothes inside, including the polka-dot dress. I'll tell him I found all of it in the back of Mum's shop buried under other bags – which is true. No one ever need know about the eBay thing. I'll email the buyer and tell them that it was all a big mistake – the polka-dot dress turned out to be a fake, and I'm really sorry but I'm not going to be posting it. Could the buyer sue me or something if I did that? I have no idea . . .

What a mess.

I arrive at the shop and go inside. Mum and Jolanta are both there, putting some 'new' stock on a rack of jeans. Two of the pairs look like the stained ones I threw in the bin when I sorted through stuff in the back. I can't believe Mum would possibly want to sell someone's tatty old jeans, washed or not. Jolanta frowns at me. Mum stops what she's doing and gives me a quick hug.

'Hi,' I say to both of them. 'I'm here to do some more work. Maybe in the back – some more sorting?' If the police do come, I might be able to dive underneath the pile of bin bags and hide out. Even the most dedicated officer might think twice before braving the back of Mum's shop. Right now, it seems like the safest option.

Mum looks at Jolanta. Jolanta stares at me smugly like a python that's just eaten a whole monkey. 'Um, Andy, can I talk to you for a second?' Mum's voice is strangely flat. 'In private.'

'Yeah, sure.'

The hairs on the back of my neck prickle. Something's up. I follow Mum to the back of the shop. Immediately I notice something different. It looks cleaner. Like instead of a hurricane hitting yesterday, it hit a week ago, and people have been trying to tidy up the wreckage. The stack of black bin bags is still there, but it's been moved to one side and piled even higher.

'Andy – Jolanta and I think that someone might have broken into the shop.'

'Broken in?' My heart judders like a blown-out tyre.

'We found some Coke cans in the recycling, and some bags that had been moved.'

'Well, if you keep a key under the mat at the back, what do you expect?' I blurt out.

Mum's jaw drops. 'So it *was* you. I mean, I didn't want to believe it.'

My mind hurtles in a thousand directions. I don't want to get in trouble. I don't want to get Thomas in trouble. How could we have been so stupid as to leave those cans in the recycling?

'You think *I* broke into the shop?' I step forward, putting my hands on my hips. Getting mad seems the only way out. '*Me*, as in your own daughter?'

'I don't know.' Mum steps back, clearly having doubts.

'I mean, seriously, Mum. Why would I do that? Do you think I came to take another pair of old jeans? A bra made out of coconuts and a dusty Hawaiian skirt? Some old wedding dress that reeks of mothballs?' Now that I've started, I can't seem to stop. 'I mean, just so you know, Mum, I can't stand most of the stuff in your shop. Especially the stuff you bring me to wear. So why did I break in – to steal the ten pounds I made for you? It's completely ridiculous and totally insulting!'

I storm out of the stockroom. As I suspected, Jolanta 'happens' to be hanging clothing on a rack right by the curtain to the back so she's heard every word.

'So that's it then,' I say. 'You want to turn my own mum against me?'

She stops what she's doing and puts her hands on her hips. 'There was a white bag in the back,' she says. 'It had some designer things in it that were left on the doorstep. I put it with the other bags – I was going to sort through it. Then you came in.' She crosses her arms. 'You threw away some perfectly good denim. And now the white bag is gone.'

'Well, it's nothing to do with me,' I say, my heart hammering in my chest. 'And if anyone left anything half-decent on the doorstep, then it was probably a mistake. I mean, why would they?' I stand up a little straighter so that I'm a good three inches taller than Jolanta.

'Girls, girls.' Mum comes in from the back. 'Look, we have to stop this now. We're a team. We have to be on the same side.'

'Do we?' I say to Mum. 'Because it seems that you two are on the same side. And you can have the shop all to yourselves. I'm leaving.'

I storm out of the shop, shaking all over. As I stand outside on the pavement, rain drips through a hole in the awning down on to my head. The cold water is like a slap in the face. I did something wrong and now I've been caught out. I know I should just go back in and confess. And if Jolanta hadn't been there, then maybe that's what

I would have done. Maybe . . .

Instead, I walk home. I find a posting bag in Mum's things in the kitchen and some tissue paper in a gift wrap box. The white bag is in my room at the bottom of the wardrobe. Mum can sort through the stuff I left in the back of the shop and find the other designer items that I didn't take. But I've sold the polka-dot dress and now I'm going to send it to the buyer and collect my £485. (Because I'm a new seller, the money won't be released from eBay to my bank account until the buyer receives the item.)

I pull the dress from the bag and give it a good shaking out. Once again I feel a little pang – the dress really is beautiful, and somewhere inside, that older, wiser part of me wishes that I could keep it for 'some day'. But the *now* part of me – the me that wears second-hand knickers and gets teased in the loos – knows that I have to do this. I fold the dress up and wrap the tissue paper around it. I've got some old Disney stickers in my desk drawer from when I was into that stuff, so I stick them on the tissue paper to keep it in place. Cinderella in her blue dress, and Belle in her yellow one. Tinkerbell waving her wand. Then I stick the package in the mailing envelope and print the address of the buyer in black pen on the front. Now it looks like any old package, my guilt tidily wrapped up in layers of paper and plastic. I'll post it tomorrow on my way to school.

I lie down on my bed, hands behind my head, elbows splayed out, staring at a brown water stain on the ceiling. On Saturday, I'll make up some excuse to Mum and get the bus into the town centre. I'll spend my £485, and it will be done. After that, I'll never do anything wrong again, I swear. I close my eyes and think about all of the things I'll buy – new jeans, a little skirt, sunglasses, T-shirts, underwear. Maybe I'll even buy a dress. Or perhaps I'll just try everything on and wait and go back a few weekends in a row, carefully making my decisions. If I 'go straight', this is all the money I'm ever going to have and I should make it last. Or maybe I'll go to a really expensive designer shop and spend the whole thing in one go. That would feel amazing, surely . . .

Because right now, when I think about my shopping trip, I feel a big gaping hole in my stomach. I don't even want to go at all. But then it would all have been for nothing. I get out of bed and put the package into the white bag, and put the bag back in the wardrobe. Do hardened criminals feel this kind of conflict and guilt?

I crawl back under the covers, wishing – more than anything – that I'd never laid eyes on the white bag and the polka-dot dress, and started down the path to the Dark Side.

12

JUDGE AND JURY

When Mum comes home, she tries to have a 'little chat', but I keep my door shut and locked. She talks through the door, saying how she would never accuse me of anything, and of course she didn't think I took anything. She was just trying to figure out if there really was a bag of nice things and, if so, what happened to it . . . I cover my ears. Finally, she goes away.

I stay in my room all evening. On her way to bed, Mum has another go, and I can tell from the strain in her voice that she's upset. I know I should open the door – I hate the way things are between us right now, and I feel really bad about what I've done, and how I've lied about it. But

I'm too scared to tell her, and besides, I know what I have to do.

When Mum's door is finally closed, I get up and take the white bag out of the wardrobe with the package inside. I tiptoe downstairs to the kitchen and find Mum's spare key – even she's probably now removed the one from under the mat behind the shop. Silently, I leave the house.

The night is dark and cloudy as I walk the ten minutes to the high street. Everything is dark, even the chippie. But when I stand in front of the old theatre and look closely, I can see the light leaking through the boards.

I go around to the alleyway and let myself into Mum's shop. I risk turning on the light so that I can dig around the pile of bin bags until I find the designer clothing I hid there. (I was worried that Mum and Jolanta might have found it already, but I guess they were looking for a white bag.) When I've found the clothing, I put it back in the white bag. I carry the bag out of the shop and lock up.

Next to the shop, the back door of the old theatre is ajar and I can hear a radio playing. Butterflies circle in my stomach as I go inside. When I reach the end of the corridor, I knock hard on the wall and call out, 'Hello?' There's no response, so I go through the curtain to the theatre.

Thomas is up on the ladder, his back to me. He's wearing old jeans and a T-shirt, both splattered with white paint. His arms are tanned and muscular. I stand and watch him for a minute as he paints a wide rectangle of wall with a roller. The music is louder in here. I call out again: 'Hey – Thomas'.

He turns around to face me. 'Hi, Andy,' he says. Then his eyes move down to the *Galeries Lafayette* bag in my hand. 'You found it!'

For a second, a way out flashes in my mind. I could just tell him I found it tonight in the shop – it got mixed in with some other things – and as far as I know, everything's there. But the lying feels like a heavy stone that I'm carrying around with me, and I can't keep doing it any longer.

'I took it,' I blurt out. I want to turn away – to avoid the frown, the accusation on his face. But I force myself not to.

He climbs down the ladder, then goes over to the radio and switches off the music. The fact he's not saying anything is even worse than if he told me off.

'I found it in the back of Mum's shop,' I say. 'It was buried under some other bags. I found your aunt's beautiful clothes. I'm totally not into vintage stuff, but I thought that they were pretty amazing.'

He doesn't speak so I blather on.

'Mum said I could have something in payment for some work I did at the shop. She thought I was taking a pair of old jeans, but really I took the polka-dot dress from the bag and hid the rest.' I sigh. Now that I've started, I know I've got to tell him the whole story. 'The thing is,' I continue, 'I really hate the fact that I have to wear somebody's old clothes all the time, and people mock me at school. I hardly ever have anything new, unless it's something my Aunt Linda sends me. I know it sounds totally lame and selfish. I was planning to go to a real shopping centre and buy some new clothes. So I took your aunt's dress and sold it on eBay.'

The words echo accusingly around the vast empty space.

'The buyer paid for it and everything. I'm supposed to post it off tomorrow.' My eyes fill with tears. 'But it's not too late to cancel the sale. I can do it first thing tomorrow. I brought the dress back too – it's in the bag.'

Thomas turns away and climbs back up the ladder. I wish he would just say something: tell me to get lost, or that he's going to call the police – anything. But he acts like I'm not even there. A minute or two goes by, and I set the bag on the floor. I should leave now. I've lost everything – the money, the nice clothes, the sale on eBay, Mum's trust, being friends with Thomas. I feel like there's nowhere I can go, no way to make things right. I look around me at the theatre. It's a beautiful place, but so run-down and shabby – just like the shop. I've ruined my chance to help out with the shop, but maybe . . .

I take off my jacket and drape it on top of the white bag. I walk over to where Thomas has his tools, pour some white paint into a spare tray, and grab a paint roller. I pick a spot about three metres away from Thomas's ladder and start painting.

I can sense him stopping his own work and watching me. I don't look at him or say anything. I've never painted a wall before, and though I try to be neat, within the first minute I manage to get flecks of white paint all over my face and top. But there's something relaxing about it. The tears in my eyes dry up. I stop thinking about what I've done. I stop thinking about Mum and Thomas. In fact, I stop thinking at all. The rectangle of paint gets larger, the wet sheen catching the light. Everything in front of me is white; the whole world is white—

'How much did you get for it?'

'Sorry?' The white world fades back to reality.

'The Chanel dress. How much?'

'Well . . .' I stare at the wall. 'Four hundred and eighty-five pounds. Before eBay fees.'

He whistles. 'That's a lot of money.'

I nod, my throat too choked up to speak.

'So when are you going on your shopping trip?'

I stop painting and look at him. 'I told you, I'm not. If you want the dress back, I'll cancel the sale. If not, then I'll send it off and give you the money as soon as I can access it.'

He's silent for a second. We both go back to our painting.

'No,' he says. 'Finders keepers. You found the bag and thought someone had dropped it off at the shop. Technically, you weren't doing anything wrong. You brought the rest of the stuff back, so you keep the money for the dress. Or give some to your mum.'

I shake my head. 'I couldn't keep the money now.'

'Whatever.' He shrugs.

We go back to painting. I think about the shopping spree that I'd planned – all the different ways I could spend the money. Money that isn't rightfully mine. But if Thomas doesn't want it, then that leaves giving it to Mum. Part of it would probably go on Jolanta's wages and the rest on sewing stuff. There must be some better use of the money than that.

I finish the wall as high as I can reach and move along, closing the gap between us. 'Why did you send the stuff to the dry-cleaners?' I say finally.

He pauses the brush in mid-stroke. 'It was stuff that had fallen off the hangers and got dusty. I thought it was nice, so I had it cleaned. It was kind of stupid really – sentimental, I guess, just like my uncle. But frankly, I can't see the point of all my aunt's stuff just hanging in a dark room.' He gives me a sideways smile. 'So maybe I'll sell it on eBay.'

'Maybe.' I'm sure he's joking.

'No, really.' He senses my disbelief. 'I could put the money towards my uni fees. When the time comes.' He turns back to the wall and continues to paint.

'Do you really want to be an architect?' I ask, remembering what his uncle said.

'It seems like a long way off,' he says. 'But I think so. I like to draw. I like old buildings – like the ones they have in Paris. I love Paris. And I'm enjoying fixing this place up.'

I look at him admiringly. While I'm flogging stuff on eBay to go shopping for clothes, he's thinking about his future.

'Wow,' I say, 'that's pretty cool.'

'What about you?' he says.

I think of the conversation I had with Stevie and Carrie. I wish I wanted to be something noble like a doctor or a scientist. But I don't. 'I'd like to run a business,' I say. The words come out of nowhere. 'Like Mum's shop – only totally different.'

'In what way?'

'Well, if I were running her shop right now, I'd make some changes. I'd start by getting rid of all the old tat – the wedding dresses and the Hawaiian outfit, the baby clothes. I'd get rid of the old jeans, and the blouses that smell like BO even when they're washed. I'd get rid of anything satin, and anything that's synthetic fabric. That stuff's OK when it's new, but it looks pretty tatty when it's not.'

'OK?'

'So basically, I'd clear everything out. I'd close the shop down for a few days, and then I'd paint the place. White – like you're doing here. And I'd get some proper fitting rooms put in. Then I'd organize the stockroom in the back – get rid of all the bin bags.'

'And then what?'

I consider this. 'Once everything was cleared out and the shop was painted, I'd sit down and figure out what the shop ought to be,' I say. 'I mean, is it just for old junk, or is it for high-end designer stuff?'

'What should it be?'

'I don't know. The polka-dot dress sold for over four hundred quid.'

'But how many of those are you going to get?'

'None.' I blush. 'I shouldn't even have had that one.'

'How are you going to get "good stuff" then?'

'I don't know . . .' I flounder. Clearing out the shop and painting it white is one thing. Getting stuff in it that will actually sell is quite another.

'Hmm.' He rubs the end of his chin. 'In Paris there are consignment stores called *dépôts-ventes*. People bring designer stuff to sell and they get a cut of the profit.'

'What do you mean?'

'Well, let's say I brought you a bag of clothes. You look through it and pick out two or three things that you want to sell in the shop. The rest is rubbish. You don't want it and I have to take it back.'

'Go on.'

'Then you write down my name on the price tag, so you know that if you sell it, it's me who gets a cut.'

'You mean like a percentage?'

'Yeah. It's your shop so you get forty per cent, but it's my stuff so I get sixty per cent.'

I roll my eyes. 'You mean, it's my shop and I'm doing the work, so I get sixty per cent. You get forty per cent. In store credit.'

He laughs. 'You drive a hard bargain, Andrea.'

I smile, liking the way he sometimes uses my whole name. No one else calls me Andrea other than his uncle.

'OK, so maybe it's sixty–forty or forty–sixty,' he says. 'You'll do some research and work out the details. In the end, hopefully you get some good stuff to sell. Then you need to get the buyers in.'

'How do I do that? I mean, maybe there'd be a chance of getting people in if we were at the other end of the high street. But this end isn't exactly Covent Garden. Though your uncle's shop gets a good crowd.'

'That's because he's good at what he does. His fish and chips are the best.'

'Right. But why wouldn't a person who's got good stuff to sell just list it on eBay? Why bring it to a shop?'

'I don't know. For some people, it's too much bother – photographing the thing, listing it, posting it. Sounds like a pain.'

'Yeah, but you're a boy.'

'You noticed, huh?' He grins.

'I noticed.' I feel my cheeks growing warm.

We both keep working, and pretty soon I've run out of paint in my tray. The open can is up near the old stage. As I walk across the vast open space, I think again about how all this is just on the other side of the wall from Mum's shop. I know that when the theatre is fixed up, Thomas and his uncle will sell it. That's the way it is, and how it should be. He stretches up to reach the top of the wall with his paintbrush. I watch him for a minute, admiring how confident and sure of himself he seems.

When he's finished the top of the wall, he climbs down the ladder. 'We'd better both go home,' he says. 'School tomorrow and all.'

'Yeah,' I say. 'You're right.' I put the lid on the open paint can and pound it down with my fist. I feel an ache inside that the evening is over.

We take the brushes and rollers to the back to clean them. When I catch a glimpse of myself in the mirror above the sink, I see that I'm completely covered in specks of white paint.

'You look like a snow queen,' Thomas says. He stares into the mirror. There's a streak of paint down his nose and his clothes have paint on them, but he's not as splattered as I am.

'Cool.' I laugh, trying hard not to blush. Seeing us there in the mirror together, I feel a little like I did when I tried on the polka-dot dress. Like I'm seeing someone I might be in a few years, but right now it's a little scary.

We finish washing out the brushes. 'It was good to get some help with the painting,' he says.

'No worries. It was fun.'

'If you ever do go ahead with the plans for the shop – you can count on me,' Thomas adds. 'For the decorating part, at least.'

'Oh,' I say, taken aback. I don't have any 'plans' and I could never just 'go ahead' with anything like we've been talking about. Could I?

He comes with me to the back door. 'If you wait for a few minutes, I'll get my things and walk you home.'

'You don't have to,' I say. 'I'll be OK. Really.'

'But it's after midnight.'

I give him a cocky smile. 'I haven't turned into a pumpkin yet, have I?'

'No.' He laughs. 'You haven't.'

He takes a step forward. Before I even know what's happening, he leans in and gives me a kiss on the cheek.

'Bye, Andy,' he says. 'See you soon.'

13

THE BIG SHOPPING TRIP

That night I don't really sleep – how could I when I've just had my first kiss? I replay it in my mind over and over – it all happened so quickly, and I know he was just being friendly, but still, a kiss is a kiss. I'm dying to tell Stevie and Carrie. (Before the incident with the white bag, I used to tell them practically everything.) But I swore to Thomas that I'd keep the secret, and I don't want to break a promise to *him*. And there's also the matter of Mum's shop. I can't stop thinking about it. All that talking rubbish – brainstorming – with Thomas has sparked loads of ideas. Given a chance, I bet I could make something of it. But how am I going to get that chance?

After school the next day, I post the polka-dot dress. I don't even feel bad doing it – well, only a *little* bad – knowing that I've come clean with Thomas and given the rest of the clothing back to him.

I leave the post office and walk to *Eliza's Emporium*. I'm dreading seeing Mum after yesterday, but I know I have to do it. I can't keep putting things off. I'm going to tell her everything.

The bell tinkles as I go inside. I'm expecting to see Jolanta sitting on the stool by the till, but instead, the entire front of the shop is empty.

'Hello?' I call out. No answer. If I was a burglar, I could just grab and go with loads of stuff. But I'd have to be a pretty lame burglar to want to steal anything that I see on the cluttered racks in front of me.

A few seconds later, Mum bustles in from the back, carrying an armful of clothing and hangers. She's wearing a billowy jungle print dress and a chunky beaded collar at the neck. She looks like a cross between an explorer and his tent.

'Hi, Andy,' Mum says. Her smile is fragile, but I appreciate the fact that she's trying to make it sound like everything's normal. 'I thought I heard the door. Sometimes it's hard when the dryer's on full tilt.'

'Where's Jolanta?' I say.

Mum sets the clothing down on top of a box marked: *odds and ends £1.* 'She's gone.'

'Gone? Gone where?'

'I mean, I let her go.'

'What?' I take a step back, stunned. 'You sacked her? But . . . you like her. And she loves the shop. I thought she was helping you.' Then a terrible thought strikes me. 'You don't think she took anything do you? That white bag? Because she didn't.' I take a long breath. 'I found the bag in the back. But then someone came by and said it was a mistake that it had been left at the shop. I gave the things back.' Tears well up in my eyes. 'I'm really sorry, Mum. Sorry that I lied. Sorry about the things I said about the shop.'

I wait for the guilty verdict. Will she ground me for the rest of my life? Ban me from the shop?

Mum sighs. She picks up a denim blouse with a rose embroidered on the pocket from the stack of clothing and puts it on a hanger. 'I knew it was too good to be true, Andy. And really, I'm the one who should be sorry. For what I've done to you – and Jolanta. I had to let her go because I couldn't afford to keep her. I can't pay someone eight pounds per hour when we barely make that all day.' She shoves the hanger on an overflowing rack. 'If things don't turn around soon, I'm going to have to close the shop.'

'Close the shop?' I feel like a very large bus has flattened the air out of my lungs. Even though I've seen the receipt book, I didn't realize things were *that* bad.

Pursing her lips, she nods. She picks up the next item and looks around the shop, as if trying to find the perfect place to put it. 'Yes, Andy,' she says quietly.

'But what will you do?' I suddenly feel panicky and short of breath. As much as I have issues with *Eliza's Emporium*, I've always thought of it as part of Mum. She's had the shop for ever; she loves it. It used to be successful; or at least, she's always had a lot of people coming in — even people who don't live close by. And now that I've started working here, I feel part of it too. 'What will *we* do?' I say.

A smile blooms on her face, almost like old times. Her bangles clank as she steps forward and ruffles my hair like I'm still a little girl. 'I'm going to take you shopping, Andy,' she says. 'If we have to liquidate, then we'll go to Westfield and buy you a whole new wardrobe. I'm sorry I didn't realize before how you felt about the shop and' — she chokes a little — 'the clothes I brought for you.

I guess vintage isn't everybody's thing.'

I feel a crushing sense of guilt that I didn't tell Mum how I felt before. Instead, I let it fester inside of me, making things bad between us. If she'd understood, then maybe things wouldn't have got this far. I never would have taken the polka-dot dress, or hidden the other things, or lied or . . . been such a terrible daughter.

'I'm so sorry, Mum,' I repeat, knowing that the words sound futile. 'Sorry that I'm always complaining and that I never help you out. I mean, not really.'

She looks at me, clearly surprised by what I've said. 'But you do help me, Andy, don't you see that? You're everything to me. Without you, I'd have nothing . . .'

I take a step forward. I want to hold her. Stroke her hair like she did for me when I was little and got upset. Tell her that everything is going to be OK, and then make that happen. But she turns away and goes back to the new stock she's brought in. She picks up a man's suit jacket from the stack, arranges it on a hanger and shoves it on to a rack.

'Mum, are you all right?' I half choke. 'I don't mean the shop or anything like that. I mean – you?'

She shakes her head, then seems to catch herself and quickly starts to nod. 'Of course, darling. I'm fine.'

I think of the gap between us that's grown over the years – mostly because of me. The rope bridge over the wide river, with dangerous waters swirling below. We're hanging on by a thread now, and it's not going to be fixed with an 'of course, I'm fine.'

'Mum, I'm not a little girl any more. If you're not OK, then you should tell me. You've always told me that we should talk about stuff. Be friends.'

She smiles. 'You're right, Andy. We should be friends. But I'm still your mum. I owe it to you to be strong. Not . . .' She trails off, like she can't trust herself to speak.

'Are you ill, Mum?' I say. 'Please – you have to tell me. It's worse not to know.'

She sighs. 'A little bit,' she says. 'But it's nothing to worry about, really.'

My blood freezes to ice. 'What is it?' I say. 'Cancer?' Of course it's cancer! It's always cancer, isn't it? Mum's going to die and I'll be an orphan. All the things I've wanted to say to her over the years, I'll never be able to say. She won't be around to see me graduate from uni, or get married. She won't be around to enjoy her grandkids or meet someone new to fall in love with herself, or grow old and enjoy a peaceful retirement. Mum's got cancer and she's going to die! I need to deal with it. I don't even notice I'm crying until I let out a great loud sob that startles both of us. 'Are you going to die?' I whisper.

'It's not cancer,' she says matter-of-factly. She picks up a pair of jeans from the stack and folds them up neatly. 'And I'm not going to die.'

'What?' I can barely hear her over the ringing in my ears. *Not cancer? Not going to die?*

'The doctor's given me some pills to help me sleep, that's all,' she says. 'And to make me feel a little brighter.' She puts the jeans on the shelf with the others.

'A little brighter? What's that supposed to mean?' Now that I know Mum's not dying, I suddenly feel really angry at her for giving me a scare like that. I wish she'd stop messing around with the new stock and the overflowing racks, and just talk to me.

'I've been suffering from depression.'

'Depression?' I draw out the word, feeling confused. 'That's it? That's why you went to the doctor?'

She gives a little laugh. 'That's it, Andy. I guess

you could say it's about the shop, though it doesn't always have a cause.'

'But . . . I mean . . . everyone gets depressed sometimes, don't they? Like being sad, or in a bad mood.'

'This is different,' she says.

'How?' I challenge. Mum's always been a happy person; a person who gets on with things. I can't believe she would let something like this cause her a problem.

She's silent for a moment. I watch as she takes a price tag on a flower-patterned shirt, crosses off the £4 that's written on it and writes – *Sale! £2.* 'I didn't want to tell you this, Andy,' she says finally, 'but sometimes I don't manage to get up in the mornings. You've already gone to school so you don't know. The shop is failing because a lot of times we aren't even open. Sometimes it's really hard for me to get through the day. I try to get on with things like normal, but I can't. Sometimes I wonder if I ought to just give up.'

'Give up? What do you mean give up? You can't just *give up*,' I practically yell. 'You've got the shop, and people who count on you. And . . . you've got me! I mean, what exactly are you saying?'

'I'm just being honest.' She turns away and

crosses out another price on a tag. 'I would never do anything to hurt you, Andy. I hope you know that.'

'Well, you are hurting me. Right now!' I kick the bottom of the rack of clothing in front of me, making the hangers rattle. A few things fall off their hangers and on to the floor. I know I'm being horribly selfish and making things worse, but I just want to take the words out of her mouth. Make them not be true.

'I'm sorry for that. And everything.' She stares at the clothing that's fallen down, like she has no idea how it got there, or what to do about it. 'I'm so . . .' A tear trickles down her cheek.

Mum's crying. I've never seen her cry before. I feel sick and scared and fascinated all at the same time. I want to do something – make her stop. I should pick up the clothing, do something to help make things better. But I just stand there, unable to move.

'So when you say "give up", what exactly do you mean? Are you going to, I don't know . . . *kill yourself?*'

'No, I mean that's not—'

'So go on, Mum,' I shout. 'What are you waiting for? Do . . . whatever depressed people do. I won't try to stop you if that's what you want.'

With a swift motion, I sweep more hangers from the rack on to the floor.

'Andy!'

'Go on. Do it. See if I care.'

I push the rack over, and run out of the shop as fast as I can.

14

THE WORST DAUGHTER IN THE WORLD

I run – down the high street, past the theatre and the shops. My ballet flats are flip-flopping off my heels, the left one rubbing a blister, but I don't care. My mum is depressed. She wants to give up. She wants to leave me here alone. Whatever I am; whatever I've done or haven't done, it's all wrong. I'm the worst daughter in the world – I must be.

I keep on going until finally I reach the edge of the village where the footpath starts across National Trust land. There's an old log just inside the stile and it's mossy and cool underneath a canopy of trees. I collapse, panting for breath.

The conversation I had with Mum churns in

my head. She didn't *actually* say she was going to kill herself – I was the one who said that. But . . . what if she does? How would she do it? I shake my head back and forth, wishing I had a remote control to turn off my mind. Mum's depressed – and I've just made things a whole lot worse.

I sit there for a while, staring at some ants marching along the log. The evening I spent painting the theatre with Thomas seems like a grainy old film of someone else's memories. The sun gradually dips lower and lower, and the shadows are long and cold. I stand up and walk slowly back towards the village. It's like I'm carrying a heavy invisible weight strapped to my back.

Back on the high street, I breathe in the aroma of fish and chips. My stomach rumbles – I haven't eaten anything since lunchtime. There are a couple of men wearing work boots and hard hats in line at the chippie, and a mum pushing a pram. I crane my neck but there's no sign of Thomas. His uncle seems to be working there all alone.

I stand behind the men as they douse their chips with vinegar and salt and finally head out of the shop. Mr LeBoeff chats amiably with the woman with the pram. I don't know what I'm doing there. I don't have any money, and when I think of Mum again, my stomach feels hollow and sick.

'Andrea,' Mr LeBoeff says, sounding happy to see me. 'It's good to see you.' He frowns. 'But you look like you need some food.'

'I don't know. I don't have any money, and besides—'

He cuts me off with a wave of his hand. 'No matter, no matter.' He heads to the back of the shop and comes back a minute later with a perfectly round, bright red apple. Smiling, he hands it to me. All of a sudden, it looks like the best thing in the world. I take it from him and hold it to my nose, then take a bite. The juicy tartness explodes in my mouth. It's delicious.

He wipes down the counter, humming tunelessly as I crunch the apple. When I finish it, he holds out his hand to take the core and throws it in a bin behind the counter.

'Thank you,' I say. 'I needed that.'

'They call this comfort food.' He gestures at the case full of fried fish and chicken goujons that are warming under the heat lamp. 'But I think that real comfort must come from within. And that means eating good food like apples.'

'Who says I need comfort?' I challenge, narrowing my eyes.

'Don't you?' He goes back to wiping and humming.

I stand there, unsure what to say; wondering how he knows what he knows. Part of me wants to walk away. But now that I'm getting to know Thomas, I feel closer to his uncle too.

'Thomas told me that you used to have a café,' I say. 'In Paris.'

Mr LeBoeff laughs, but I see that sad look in his eyes that I've noticed before. 'We never know where life will take us,' he says. 'All we can do is be ready to follow the path.'

'He also mentioned your wife. That she . . . um . . . I'm sorry.'

He frowns, rubbing hard at a non-existent mark on the stainless steel.

'Hélène had cancer,' he says. 'Which ultimately took her life. But things were difficult for her even before that. We couldn't have children of our own. And then, in the same year, Thomas's parents died and she began to get sick.'

'They died?' The blood chills in my veins. I've never really talked to Thomas before the other night, and I still don't know much about him. But I guess I'd always just assumed that he lived with his parents somewhere in the village and had a part-time job at his uncle's shop.

'What happened?' I can't stop myself asking.

'Hélène's brother Marc – Thomas's father – and his wife were killed in a car accident in Paris,' he says. His eyes turn liquid with unshed tears. 'It was . . . terrible. You can't even imagine.'

'No. I can't. I'm so . . .' I trail off. 'Sorry' just sounds wrong.

'It is not something that one can ever *get over*. But one must get on with life. Hélène and I took it upon ourselves to raise the boy. We came here to be near Hélène's sister and her family.'

'But what about your lives in Paris? I mean, it must have been hard giving that up.'

'For her, yes. So many people loved her, and yet, I suppose, it was not enough. Hélène was like that. She had a . . . sadness inside her sometimes. A part of her that I could never reach. That year, she became unable to work. Leaving was for the best. It gave me time to focus on her, and the boy. Help them both through the difficult time.'

I nod, not knowing what to say. He's suffered so many tragedies, and yet he's got on with things; managed to remain positive. Though, according to Thomas, there's a part of him that's still stuck in the past.

He sighs. 'When someone you love is suffering, being there for them is all you can do. You may feel powerless to help, but that is when they need you the most.'

And this time when he looks at me, I get the idea that we're no longer talking about his wife. I recall that day at the shop, when he asked after Mum. He had seemed so serious, so concerned. It dawns on me that maybe this man whom I barely know saw what I didn't see in my own mum – didn't, or didn't want to.

I cross my arms, suddenly feeling defensive. 'Why are you telling me this?'

He goes back to wiping down the counter. 'Your mother used to come into my shop some-times. We would talk – after all, we are neighbours. I liked the way she used to laugh; the way she was so passionate about her business. And of course, I know that she suffered the loss of your father.'

'It was a long time ago,' I say. Mum never really talks about Dad, but I know she still misses him.

'Yes, but even so.' He shakes his head. 'I don't pretend to know her well, but lately I have not seen her so much. And when I do, she seems changed.' His eyes are deep and reflective as he looks up at me. 'She no longer laughs. She no longer has that sparkle about her.'

The laughing, the sparkle – I haven't thought

of it in those terms, but I know that he's spot on. How could I have been so selfish not to have noticed? Not to have tried to *do* something?

'Perhaps I should keep quiet – not tell this to you. If that is the case, Andrea, then I am sorry.' He shakes his head. 'But I don't think anyone gets to the end of their life and thinks: *I wish I'd done less.* No, one always wishes that they had done *more.* Showed more compassion and understanding. Been less afraid.'

The more he talks, the more I feel like I'm tangled up in knots. 'Well, it's really none of your business, is it?' I lash out.

Mr LeBoeff smiles sadly. 'No, of course not. But Andrea – please. Go and be there for her. Go and help her. You are her daughter and you are kind and loving. Together you can get through this.'

'Just leave me alone, OK?' My heart is pounding as I leave the chippie and walk slowly down the pavement until I'm out of sight.

Then I start running as fast as I can back towards home.

15

BUT SHE STILL DOESN'T GET IT . . .

By the time I get home, my hand is shaking so hard that I can barely turn my key in the door. The television is on in the front room. I feel so scared – I can barely bring myself to come inside. What if Mum's already given up? Or . . . worse . . . ?

I lean against the door frame, my breath coming in gasps. Then I hear another sound. A rustling, and then the sound of crunching. I poke my head into the room. Mum is sitting on the sofa, eating her way through a bag of Doritos, watching a repeat episode of *Holby City*.

'Mum?' I say in a strangled voice. Tears begin to roll down my cheeks.

She looks up and smiles, then does a double-take. 'Andy? Are you OK?'

I rub the tears away with my fist. 'I thought you . . . I mean, I was worried that . . .'

She mutes the television and gets up from the sofa. The next moment I'm lost in an endless hug. Her hair tickles my cheek, I breathe in a hint of sandalwood and rose, and it's like coming home after a long, tiring journey. I don't want my mum to give up. I don't want her to have to close the shop. Whatever it takes, I'm going to make sure that Mum's OK.

'I shouldn't have run out like that,' I say, gasping out the words. 'I should have been there for you. And I wasn't. I'm so sorry, Mum.'

She holds me at arm's length and wipes the lines of tears from my cheeks. 'Darling, Andy. Please – let's talk about this. I thought it was best to be honest with you about how I've been feeling. I had no idea you were going to get so upset. You don't have to feel guilty.'

I let her lead me by the hand like a lost child. She sits me down on the sofa and perches on the edge of the threadbare wing chair that she found in a skip somewhere and reupholstered. She picks up the bag of crisps. 'Dorito?' she asks.

'Thanks.' I don't really want one, but I take one anyway.

Mum sits back in the chair, the wooden frame creaking with her weight. 'Depression is an illness,' she says. 'It's caused by a chemical imbalance in the brain. It's not me just making it up or feeling sorry for myself.' Her speech sounds too polished and proper – like someone else has prepped her. 'And it can be treated. So the doctor says anyway.' Her smile looks brittle. 'I'm going to be taking medication. It's called an SSRI – a serotonin something-or-other. And I'm on a waiting list for therapy – to talk to someone.'

I try to take in what she's saying and feel OK about it. She's going to be taking pills; she's going to talk to someone; she's going to be fine. But I feel like there's a hole that's opened up inside me. I wish Mum didn't have an illness, but if she has to have one, I kind of wish it was one that seemed a little more real – more normal. Something everyone else would understand . . .

'But you don't have to go to . . . you know . . . like a mental hospital?' I can barely get the words out.

She laughs – something I haven't heard in a long time. 'No, Andy.' She takes my hand and squeezes it. 'I promise I'm not going anywhere.'

'OK, Mum.' I squeeze her hand back and try to laugh too. But it comes out more like a sob.

'I just need to start taking the pills,' Mum explains again. 'They take a few weeks to work – to rebalance things. And I may feel tired, or groggy, or irritable. I'm sorry if that's the case. But the doctor says they should work. Lots of people take them for short periods, just to get things back on track.'

'And what then? What about the shop?'

Her face falls, and I realize that all the stuff about medication and therapy is an act. It's the shop that's the problem. And because she loves it, I don't want her to lose it.

'The doctor says that what's happening with the shop is my "trigger". It's, like, the thing that caused me to start feeling low in the first place.'

'Yeah, I get that.'

'It's just been so hard lately. Getting up. Going to work. Going through the motions. I've been feeling really drained – like everything is a struggle. But I'm going to be fine.' She reaches over and tries to fluff my hair like I'm a baby. I lean away, then think the better of it and let her.

'How do you know you'll be OK?' I say. 'I mean, it's all good and well to say that.'

She gives a little laugh. 'Well, I'm hoping that I'll have more energy. Be back to my old self. Once the pills kick in, that is. Then I'll be fine going back to the shop. I need to change the window display anyway for summer. And I was thinking that I could put an advert for the shop in the council magazine.'

'I guess that might be a start,' I say. 'Especially the window display part. I like the black dress on, um . . . "Amelie".'

'Yes, that is stylish, isn't it?' She smiles. 'I'll change the display, and then I'll go through all the bags in the back – put out as much stock as I can . . .'

No. I catch myself before the word comes out. The last thing *Eliza's Emporium* needs is more of the same stuff. But how can I make Mum see what I see?

'Um, maybe I can help you out in the shop some more,' I say, seizing the moment. 'I had a few ideas myself about how to make it better. Like, maybe you need to have less stock rather than more. Just put out the good stuff? Then people can see what's there on the racks. And also, you could raise the prices.'

This time, it irritates me when Mum laughs. I knew she wouldn't listen to my ideas about the shop.

'Thanks, Andy. But I've been doing this for a long time. I think I know the best way to turn things around. And you need to focus on school. Get good marks, do well in your exams when the time comes. You're smart, Andy. You can go to uni. You can make something of your life. Don't end up like me.'

'Don't be so hard on yourself, Mum. I mean, you're so creative. And you know so much about . . . uh . . . vintage stuff. Your customers seem to love coming in and talking to you. That's a really good thing, I think.'

She smiles gratefully. I notice that there are wrinkly lines around her eyes that I swear weren't there before. She *does* looks drained . . . worn out.

An idea strikes me.

'I think it's great that you want to make the shop better,' I say. 'And I'm sure you've got a lot to be getting on with. But maybe before you start you should have a break. You could think through exactly what you want to do. Get some rest. Take time to get better.'

'A break?' She frowns like I'm speaking a foreign language.

'You know, like a holiday.'

'A holiday?' She looks horrified. 'But I couldn't.'

'Just think about it,' I say, as the roots of a plan take hold in my mind.

16

SELF-IMPROVEMENT

All that weekend, I'm still worrying about Mum. I stay in, tidy my room, do the laundry, try to be a better daughter – one who would have noticed earlier how bad Mum was feeling. Until the tablets start working, I guess she'll still be feeling bad, and who knows what might happen? By Sunday night, I'm more and more convinced that a holiday is just the thing she needs. A holiday far away from here. But how can I get her to do it?

On Monday, I make her an extra-special breakfast of an egg and soldiers, like she used to make me when I was sick. I take it up to her room on a tray, along with a cup of strong coffee.

She's still in bed, looking pale and groggy. Her

eyes have red rims around them like she hasn't slept that well. But when I enter the room, she brightens.

'Andy, that's so thoughtful of you!'

I force myself to smile cheerfully, and set the tray down on the rumpled duvet. 'How are you feeling, Mum?'

'Fine,' she says with a yawn. 'Just a little tired. Maybe it's the tablets.' She leans over and looks at the clock, frowning. 'You'd better hurry up or else you'll be late for school.'

'Um, yeah. I'm off now. But . . .' I hesitate. Mum still seems so flat and lacking in energy. Now that I know the truth, it seems blindingly obvious. Mr LeBoeff noticed it, and he hardly knows her, whereas I'm her daughter. How did I miss it for all these months? '. . . but you're going to be OK today?' I say. 'On your own?'

Mum downs a long sip of coffee. 'Andy, I'm fine. Really. I'm not going to do anything silly.'

'OK, Mum.' I guess I have to take her word for it. I lean over and give her a kiss. 'Love you,' I say.

'I love you too.' She smiles, and for a second I catch a glimpse of her the way she used to be. That makes me feel a little better. Still, as I leave the room and go off to school, the hole in my stomach is filled with worries.

I find it hard to concentrate on learning about the Norman Conquest, adverb phrases and the anatomy of a frog. The day drags on, and my mind keeps flipping back to Mum and whether or not she's OK. Did she get out of bed? Did she open the shop? By the afternoon, I'm itching to go and check on her. But I have one more class first – 'Learning about the World'.

We all shuffle into the room and take our seats. Ms Cartwright is at the front of the room with her laptop, and there are some slides up on the big screen about the similarities and differences between the Jewish, Christian and Muslim religions, and about the fighting in the Middle East. But I'm less interested in the lesson than in her outfit – today it's a red brocade pencil skirt, a fuzzy black cardigan, black tights and toffee apple-red heels. As she paces back and forth in front of the class, I wonder if any of the things she's wearing came from Mum's shop.

She ends the lecture five minutes early to give us a new assignment. 'For the rest of this term we're going to be focusing on self-improvement,' she says. 'I want each of you to come up with a project that will make something about your life better.' She looks at each one of us in turn.

When her eyes land on me, I can't help but blush a little.

'It can be anything you want – from tidying your room, to helping out more with chores around the house, to learning a new skill – anything. But you need to make a plan and follow it through.' There's a general whispering and rustling of papers. I hear snickering from a couple of boys at the back of the room.

'I'd like you to prepare an outline of your proposal,' Ms Cartwright says. 'Your mark will depend on how well you articulate your goals, and how well you achieve them. I'll go through them with you, to help you put your ideas together.'

The bell rings and everybody scrambles out of class. I wait for everyone else to leave, and walk out slowly with Stevie and Carrie to go to our lockers.

'I can't believe that Ms Cartwright actually came up with something interesting for us to do,' Stevie says, sounding upbeat. 'Now I can learn to walk *and* get credit for it at school.'

'Are you still in pain?' When I'd rung Stevie after her first lesson, to ask how it went, she'd been so tired that she could barely talk. I'd felt really proud of her, but worried too.

'My arms still hurt like anything,' she says. 'It was like trying to lift a corpse. I really need to pump up my biceps to get stronger.' She flexes her skinny arm. 'I need to wheel myself more, not use the motor. Then, once I can support myself on the treadmill, my legs can kind of walk by themselves to develop the muscles.'

'Cool.' I say. 'How long is it going to take?'

'I'm not sure,' Stevie says. 'They said six months before I take my first steps. But there are no guarantees. What about you, Carrie?'

Carrie sighs. 'I guess it's a no-brainer what my special project needs to be,' she says. 'Get fit, lose weight, spend "quality time" with my dad. How many kilos should I write down to lose – five? Ten?'

'Too bad the kilos can't go over to me.' Stevie wrinkles her nose. 'I need to bulk up if I'm going to be able to walk.'

'I think your project should be standing up to your dad,' I say to Carrie. 'Tell him you're fine the way you are. If you need to bond, then do something fun – something *you* want to do.'

Carrie rolls her eyes. 'He thinks it *is* fun. When we did the 3k run yesterday, he barely even broke a sweat. I was drenched. And then we had this big bean stew for lunch – which he loved. I hate beans.' She slumps against her locker. 'But I guess I could do with getting a bit fitter.' She smiles at Stevie. 'Maybe we can do some weights together.'

'Maybe,' Stevie says. 'What about you, Andy?'

'Well . . . I've got an idea too. And actually, it might help both of your projects.' I smile. 'It's going to take some muscle. But it will be fun too.'

'Oh.' Carrie leans forward. 'What is it?'

'I'm going to transform my mum's shop.'

I'm half expecting drum rolls to come out of nowhere, but of course, nothing happens.

'Into what?' Stevie asks.

'Into a totally cool, totally retro consignment shop – like they have in Paris. A *dépôt-vente.*' I try to put on the accent. 'Selling only top-class designer stuff. Like Chanel. No more tatty old jeans and fancy dress rubbish.'

Carrie raises an eyebrow. 'A *dépôt*-what?'

'*Vente* – I think.'

'And your mum is OK with you doing it?' Stevie asks.

I shrug. 'I didn't say I've worked out all the details. But here's the thing . . .' I tell them that Mum's been feeling bad, and that I'm really worried about her. Once I get started, I find that I can't stop. I even tell them about the tablets, and the illness – depression.

'Gosh, Andy, I had no idea,' Carrie says.

'Neither did I – I mean, not really. I guess it was easier *not* to notice. Apparently, the shop is her "trigger" for feeling low. So if I could turn it around, then that would help her.'

'That sounds good,' Stevie says. 'So where do we come in?'

That part I do know. And I tell them my plan.

17

LORD SUGAR, EAT YOUR HEART OUT

When I write everything down that evening in an outline for class, it comes to three whole pages. I make bullet points: the clear-out, getting rid of the tatty stock, painting the shop, and then the consignment idea that Thomas and I talked about. But there's one thing on the very first page that I don't have a clue how I'm going to do. It's the 'convince Mum' bullet point. I think about all the things I could say to her: it's a project for school, it's Thomas's idea, it's Stevie and Carrie's idea. Because if I tell her that I came up with the plan myself, I worry that she'll just laugh at me like she did before, and start talking about GCSEs and uni. And she'll want to control the whole thing. She'll go with her ideas – things like adding more stock and lowering the prices. Ideas that aren't going to turn things around.

I know it's her shop, and I want to make her happy, not more upset. But I'm just itching to get on with my plan – my *vision* – which is 'out with the old and in with the new' (even if the 'new' is still second-hand, but high-end designer stuff that sells for more money). I just know it could work, and that Mum would love it. But with her around, it seems impossible.

I take a new sheet of paper and jot down Plan B – 'Operation Mum Holiday'. If I could get Mum to take a break for a few days – or weeks – I could get on with making a difference. (And I really believe she'll feel much better if she got away for a little bit and cleared her head.) I think about how Thomas is painting the theatre without his uncle knowing about it, or having his permission. He's doing it as a labour of love, for his uncle's own good. But Mr LeBoeff never visits the old theatre, whereas Mum is at her shop every day.

There's only one person I can think of who might be able to help – Aunt Linda. After dinner, when Mum's watching TV and fixing some beading that's come off an old prom dress, I find her number in Mum's address book. Keeping my voice low, I call her from upstairs. It's kind of awkward at first – she immediately suspects that I'm calling because I want something. After a minute or so of small talk, I cut to the chase. 'Um, Aunt Linda,' I say, 'I wanted you to know that there are some things going on with Mum . . .' I break off and swallow hard, trying to keep from crying. 'And I'm not really sure what to do.'

Pulling myself together, I tell her that Mum hasn't been feeling well in herself, and that I'm really worried about her. I'm not surprised to discover that Mum hasn't told her sister anything about how she's feeling – certainly not about the depression and the tablets. Although they talk every week, I know Mum likes to give the impression that things are going well, even when they're not. Aunt Linda immediately gets her knickers in a twist over the whole thing, and I feel little prickles of guilt that I've gone behind Mum's back. *It's for her own good*, I remind myself.

'I'll come right down for a visit,' Aunt Linda says. 'Let me just check my diary and make some arrangements.'

'Actually,' I say quickly, 'I thought that maybe we could come up and see you. Mum hasn't had a holiday in a long time. She's always at the shop, she hardly ever gets out. I was thinking that a change of scene might really help her.'

'Hmm,' she mulls. 'I see what you mean.'

'I know she really misses the Lakes,' I say. 'And you and Grandma.' (Both true!) 'It might be nice for her to do some hillwalking or whatever. Like when you were kids . . .'

Mum and her sister grew up in Kendal in the Lake District. Their mum waited on tables in a tea room, and their dad hired boats out on Lake Windermere. As far as I know, she had a happy childhood. Mum moved to London to go to fashion college, and met my dad, and Aunt Linda took over running the tea room. Now she owns it. When I was little we used to go up to the Lake District for a week every summer. I have happy memories of those times. Aunt Linda's home-made chocolate mint cake was to die for, and I also enjoyed going around to all the twee little souvenir shops with Mum so that she could check the half-price racks for things for the shop. Just about everything she bought was some kind of fleece or tartan – skirts, scarves, socks, even gloves – but at least it was all new. I can still remember the way those shops smelled – of locally made fudge, new wool and vanilla candles. Never fuggy or old.

I try to remember how long it's been since we last went there. Probably three or four years at least. Mum talks to her sister regularly, and to her mum – my grandma – maybe once a month. The more I think about it, the more I'm convinced that a visit to the Lake District could be just what Mum needs. And it would be great for my plans.

'It would be lovely to see you both,' Aunt Linda says, bringing me out of my thoughts. 'But don't you have school?'

'Yeah. But if Mum comes up on her own, I can easily stay with my friend Stevie down here.'

My aunt draws a sharp breath. 'Not a boy?'

'Oh no.' I sputter a laugh. 'Sorry, her real name is Alice. She's a girl, don't worry. Or I have another friend – Carrie. We all do our homework together anyway. It would be no trouble.'

'Why don't you and your mum just come up at Easter?' Aunt Linda sounds suspicious now.

I hesitate, my brain twisting upside down. It was supposed to be a secret, but I'm starting to think that I need as many people on side as possible. 'Well, Aunt Linda, actually, there's a reason why Mum needs to come up sooner rather than later.'

It takes me a breathless five minutes to explain my idea (emphasizing the school project angle for

Ms Cartwright's class). I need Mum out of here so that I can give the shop a makeover. 'I've got a few friends that are going to help me,' I say. 'I'm even writing a business plan.'

Of course, Aunt Linda immediately finds the one problem with the whole thing. 'You're thirteen years old,' she says. 'I'm sure you have lots of good ideas, but this isn't something you can do on your own.'

Why not? I'm about to say. But I stop myself just in time. I need to sound grown-up if I'm going to convince her.

'Maybe it takes a fresh pair of eyes to really make a difference,' I say, using one of Ms Cartwright's favourite expressions.

The phone clicks against Aunt Linda's earring – she's obviously shaking her head. 'I admit that what you say has a lot of merit,' she says. 'It's been a while since I've been to visit, but from what I remember, *Eliza's Emporium* does need a major overhaul. Clearing it out and starting again isn't a bad idea. But why don't you get your mum on board to help you?'

I give her my reasons – Mum would never accept clearing out and starting again. 'Otherwise, she would have done it already,' I say. I tell her about the time Mum spends altering some of the clothes – like the cardigan with the funky buttons – and then sells them for practically nothing. 'She wants to cram in even more stock,' I say. 'Which isn't the answer.'

'Hmm,' Aunt Linda says when I've finished. All I can do is cross my fingers and wait for her decision.

'Let me talk to Eliza,' Aunt Linda says. 'I'll find out if she wants to come up and if she would be happy for you to stay with a friend.'

'OK – great.'

'I'll ring her tomorrow. And, Andy – don't worry about anything. We'll get her through this.'

'Yeah, thanks for your help. And, um . . . what about the shop?'

'I'll think about what you said. For now, I won't mention it.'

'Thanks,' I say, my chest starting to fizz. It's not exactly a result, but I've done the best I can.

18

IN THE DANCE HALL . . .

The next evening, Carrie and I go over to Stevie's to do our homework. After dinner, I tell them about the business plan I wrote, and about the call I had with Aunt Linda.

'So you don't know if she's going to help you?' Carrie asks.

'I think she will.' I try to sound hopeful. 'But I'll have to wait and see. Anyway, I should go now. I've still got some things I need to work out.'

'OK,' Stevie says, looking doubtful. 'Good luck.'

Outside, the sky looks like turquoise velvet, and a few stars are visible above the horizon. I walk along the high street towards Mum's shop. There's a line of customers in front of the chippie. But Thomas told me that he has Tuesday nights off. I'm hoping I know where he'll be.

There's no music coming from inside the old theatre, but the door to the back alleyway is ajar. It creaks when I open it, and all of a sudden my cheek starts to tingle as I remember The Kiss. *He was just being friendly*, I scold myself. Still . . .

'Thomas?' I call. I walk to the end of the corridor and through the velvet curtain.

The vast space is empty, but he's clearly been busy. The wall we were working on together is done, and he's also started on the far wall that goes along the street. In one corner is a whole stack of new paint cans ready and waiting.

I walk to the centre of the space, imagining how it must have looked back in the day: the band on stage lit with coloured lights, men in uniform on leave from the war, whirling around, their sweethearts wearing dresses with full skirts – like the polka-dot dress – bright red lipstick, and Mary Jane shoes. I once saw a film called *Swing Kids* when I was over at Stevie's house. Those kids were amazing dancers – doing throws and lifts and dips – the jitterbug, I think it was called. I close my eyes and spin around slowly, imagining. I can almost hear the music in my head, feel the ghosts coming out of the corners of the room after so many years of being forgotten—

'Andy?'

I let out a little squeak of surprise.

'May I have this dance?' he says with a grin. He takes my right hand in his left and puts his other hand on my waist. My heart is beating so hard that I'm sure he must be able to hear it. He slowly begins to lead me in a circle. He sweeps me around, humming softly, and then lets go of my waist and spins me under his arm. Even though I've never danced before, I somehow manage to find the rhythm. The ghosts are there, just beyond the circle of us, watching, urging us to keep going.

He spins me out and I stumble over my feet. He grabs my arm and together we teeter there in mid-air until I collapse on my bottom. For a second we both look at each other, shocked. And then burst out laughing. He pulls me to my feet.

'*Merci, mademoiselle*,' he says with a little bow. 'That was a, um ... lovely ... dance.'

'I was terrible, you mean!' I say, wiping a tear of laughter from my eye.

'OK, well, maybe we ought to stick to painting,' he says. 'Because there's still a whole lot to do. And the ceiling needs two coats.'

*

Maybe I've let the ghosts down, but after laughing like that, I feel better than I have in a long time. It feels good to have a friend like Thomas who's so . . . different from my other friends. We get out the paint and I work on the wall while Thomas climbs up to the top of the ladder and starts the ceiling. Tiny droplets of paint float down to the floor like snow.

'This is gonna take for ever.' His arm muscles flex as he holds up the two-metre roller and does another tiny swathe of ceiling. Paint dusts his face with a sheen of white.

I paint a glistening white rectangle on the wall in front of me, enjoying making it bigger and bigger. I'm glad that the theatre is so large – so that we can keep doing this. I wish we *could* make the painting last for ever. As I work, I try to be brave enough to broach the thing that's been on my mind ever since I wrote the business plan for class.

'Did you tell your uncle what you're doing to the place?' I ask, finally. It's as good an opening line as any.

'Not yet,' he says. 'I want to finish the painting before getting the estate agent in. It will look more impressive that way.'

I pause in my painting and turn towards him. 'I was thinking ... I mean – have you thought about keeping the place? Doing something with it yourself?'

'Me?' He gives me a look. 'What could I do?'

'Well, I know it sounds kind of crazy, but I had this idea ...'

I tell him the whole thing.

19

LA BELLE HÉLÈNE

For the next five minutes, I don't even stop to breathe. I tell him about this crazy vision I've come up with – of a huge designer clothing boutique in the old theatre. *Eliza's Emporium* the way it could – and should – be. The more I talk, the clearer it becomes. The sparkling mirrors, the racks of beautiful clothing. Customers coming from far and wide just for a browse. Then I tell him about my school project, and how I'm hoping Aunt Linda can convince Mum to take a holiday. I tell him that Mum's feeling bad about the shop, but that she doesn't seem to get that her ideas aren't enough. And every time I falter, every time I start thinking that the whole thing sounds insane, I take a breath and think about how I felt when I tried on the polka-dot dress. I try to think about what that older, more confident me – the one I could be some day – might say. And then I say it.

'Wow,' he says, when I finally stop talking. 'That sounds like quite a project.'

'I know it's a little bit crazy. But I'd start small – redo Mum's shop and go from there.'

He gives me a look that might be respect – or pity; I can't quite tell. 'I get that,' he says, 'but even if you start small, you're talking about relaunching a whole business. How are you going to get this "new stock" you're talking about?'

I frown, a little annoyed that he's not more *can do* about the whole thing.

'I don't know,' I say. 'I've still got the eBay money from the dress.' *Your aunt's dress*, I don't add. 'That ought to cover the paint and stuff. And I'm going to do all the work myself.'

'Ah.' His blue-grey eyes twinkle. 'You're not, though, are you? I'm sure you'll *manage* to find some help.'

'Well, I might have been hoping to find a few volunteers.' I smile.

He's silent again as he moves the ladder, climbs back up, and does another white strip on the ceiling with the roller. I turn back to the rectangle I've painted on the wall. It strikes me how lame I must sound, going on like that. Who am I to talk about *visions* and *relaunching* a business? What do I know about getting stock, or customers, or real fashion? Nothing. A week ago, all I wanted to do was get some pocket money so I could buy some new clothes. And now I'm talking about redoing Mum's whole shop and expanding it into the theatre too. I shake my head, wishing I could erase the last five minutes of thinking aloud. As everyone keeps pointing out – I'm only thirteen.

'I think Hélène would have liked you.' His voice is so quiet that I wonder if he's talking to himself.

'What's that?'

'My aunt. Her name was Hélène, but in Paris she was known as "La Belle Hélène".' He stares down at the floor. 'That means, "The Beautiful Hélène".'

'Oh.'

'I don't remember her that well, but my uncle still talks about her a lot. I've got a pretty good idea of her in my mind. For some reason, I always picture her here.'

'Your uncle bought the theatre for her, right?'

'Yeah. They'd been through a hard time, but

like I said, my uncle's always really positive. They were going to make a new start. Hélène loved the theatre, so he bought it for her. He says that she had a *vision* for what to do with it. I think she wanted to open a design school here when she got well.' He dips his roller back in the paint. 'But she didn't get well so it never happened.'

'That's so sad.' I think about Thomas losing his parents – he hasn't mentioned them, and he probably doesn't remember much about them either. He must have been about the same age I was when my dad died – and I have very few memories of him. But to Mr LeBoeff, the memories must live on. It would have been nice if Hélène had been able to see out her dream before she died. But I guess that's not how life works.

'It is sad,' Thomas says. I sense that he's eager to change the subject. 'But anyway,' he adds, 'I don't think a design school would have worked. I mean, it must cost a fortune to set up a school. You can't do it just like that.'

'Plus there's already a design college near here.' I tell him about Jolanta's college. 'It's a good school. Mum says the kids are talented.' I go back to painting my rectangle. 'But it's expensive. Most of them have jobs in retail. I know that Jolanta and some of her friends also sell the stuff they make at a market stall.'

'A market stall? That's hardly likely to earn them much money.'

'I guess everyone has to start somewhere.'

'Hmm.' He sets down his roller. For a second I think he's going to say it's time to call it a night. Instead, he gestures to me to follow him. 'Let's take a break. I want to show you something.'

I follow him to the back of the theatre, down the corridor with the dressing rooms. He washes his hands in the basin and I do the same. Then he opens up a cupboard above the sink. There's a key ring hanging inside the door. He takes it and leads me back out into the corridor. Opposite the bathroom, there's a door painted in chipped black gloss secured with a heavy padlock. He finds the right key and opens the lock.

The door squeaks when he pushes it open. He flicks on a light switch and a bank of fluorescent lighting flickers on. The whole room is filled with clothing racks and white canvas bags hanging off wooden coat hangers.

'What is this stuff?' I say. 'The costumes?'

'Not exactly.'

Thomas goes over to the first rack. He unzips one of the bags and takes out what's inside.

I gasp. The sleeveless dress on the hanger is

made from a white material so fine and transparent that it seems like spider's webs. From the draped cowl neckline to the floaty zigzagged hem, it's covered with a million tiny glittering crystals. Even in the bad lighting, the dress is so sparkly that it practically glows.

'Amazing,' I say.

'This dress was made in the 1920s by a French designer called Madeleine Vionnet,' Thomas says. 'It's almost a hundred years old, and in perfect condition.'

'It should be in a museum,' I say.

'Maybe,' he says. Already he's zipping open the next bag. 'This is a Valentino.' He holds up a little black dress with a shocking white collar shaped like a folded paper fan. 'Hélène modelled lots of his stuff.'

The next bag has another sparkly ballgown that belongs at the BAFTAs or the Oscars. The one after that has a tailored black suit with buttons shaped like the Chanel 'C' logo. I've never seen such a treasure trove of beautiful clothing in my life.

'This stuff is amazing,' I say.

'Yeah. Hélène had lots of stuff from modern designers that she worked with, but she also collected clothing from the past. One-of-a-kind vintage pieces.'

'And all along it's been hidden just behind the wall from Mum's shop.' I shake my head in wonder.

Thomas laughs. 'It *is* ironic, isn't it?'

'And it must be really valuable.'

'You'd need every penny if you're going to make *your* vision happen.'

I frown. 'What do you mean?'

'I was thinking that you could sell some of it on eBay, like you did with the polka-dot dress. You could take a percentage.'

'But . . .'

'Don't worry, I'm not being that generous. What was the split we agreed – sixty–forty?'

I gulp. 'Forty–sixty. But in this case, I think I could give you a special deal.'

'I would hope so.'

'But . . . I mean, you can't just sell them. Can you?'

'I'm not a woman, so I'm not going to be wearing them, am I?'

'But your uncle – surely he must be keeping them for a reason.'

Thomas shrugs. 'What good are they doing him?'

'Maybe nothing. But Mum has lots of clothes that have "sentimental value". Things she can't bear to part with because she remembers wearing them on special occasions. Like her birthday, or ... you know ... places she went with my dad when he was alive.'

'I get that.' He crosses his arms. 'But we're not talking about a couple of dresses. My aunt got tonnes of free clothing from the designers she worked with. Shoes, handbags, the lot. We could start with some of that stuff. There's no point in keeping everything.'

'But how will we know what your uncle wants to keep unless we ask him?'

'Look, Andy.' He crosses his arms. 'If you're not in, then that's fine. I'll do it myself. It'll all have to go anyway, when the theatre's sold. I'll get some-one in to price the whole lot – probably for a lot less than it's worth – and they can just get rid of it.'

He's testing me – but I've no idea what's a pass and what's a fail. 'Fine.' I try to sound nonchalant. 'If you really want to sell some of it, then I'm in. But I think you should tell your uncle.'

'Did you tell your mum about the polka-dot dress?'

'Well ... no. Not yet.'

'No, not yet,' he repeats. His eyes lock with mine – a clear challenge.

'But I'm going to,' I say, refusing to flinch. 'Eventually.'

'That's one of the things I like about you, Andy,' Thomas says, his face breaking into a grin. 'We think so much alike.'

20

THE PLAN IN ACTION . . .

Thomas and I may think alike, but Mum and I might as well be from different planets. All of a sudden, she seems determined to turn things around all on her own – which should be a good thing. But it *so* isn't. When I get home, she's going through a bag of clothes that even a charity shop would probably reject. She's putting a price tag on every faded Babygro, bobbly jumper, holey pair of jeans and pair of grass-stained trainers.

'Have you spoken to Aunt Linda?' I say, feeling desperate. 'About maybe having a holiday? A change of scene?'

Mum sniffs. 'I can't afford to take a holiday, Andy. I've got so much stuff to do. I'm going give the shop a good clear-out.'

'So you're going to get rid of stuff?' I perk right up.

She gives me an exasperated look. 'That "stuff" is my "stock",' she says. 'I'm going to get rid of it by selling it. I'm going to have a big sale. Now that it's spring, I can move some of the racks outside.'

'But what if no one wants to buy it?' I point to the stack of baby clothes she's put carefully to one side. 'I mean, if you had a baby, would you want it to wear that?'

Mum sighs and puts her head in her hands. All the brightness seems to have gone out of her. 'Andy, you're really not helping at all. I'm trying to be positive and find some direction. Something that will save us. And all you do is put me down.'

'I'm sorry you think that, Mum!' I *am* trying to be encouraging but everything seems to come out all wrong. 'I'm glad you're having a go at turning things around. It's just that I've got some ideas that might help too. Like getting rid of the old stock that isn't selling. And raising the prices for the best pieces and the things you've altered by hand – your "finds".' I pray that just this once she'll see sense.

Mum shakes her head. 'I'm sure you have lots of good ideas, Andy. But this is business. You're thirteen years old – focus on school, and some day, when you're older, I'm sure you can teach me a thing or two.'

I swallow hard. She's not going to listen, and anything I say is bound to make things worse. But the more I hear about Mum's plans, the more I feel I have to *do* something. I understand why Thomas doesn't want to tell his uncle what he's doing – it's so easy for a grown-up to come in and ruin everything just because they can. But he's getting on with his project, and I need to do whatever it takes to get on with mine.

'Yeah, Mum, I understand,' I say. 'It's just, when I picked up the call from Aunt Linda the other night, I got a little bit worried. It sounded, um . . . like something was wrong.' I justify the lie by the fact that it's *for her own good*.

'What?' Her face goes pale. 'Is something wrong with Mum?'

'I don't know,' I say. 'I think she just thought it might be nice if you went up there.'

'God, I'm such a terrible person,' she says. 'I never go up there and visit my own mother – or my sister. I'm so selfish, and a failure at everything. I couldn't stand it if something was wrong with Mum.'

'Mum . . .' I can't stand to hear her talking like

this, especially since it's my lie that's upset her. 'You're not a failure, and you're definitely not selfish. But maybe you should go up there for a few weeks. Then you could come back and get a new start on things with the shop.'

'A few weeks?' She looks horrified.

'You always said spring was the best time to visit the Lakes.'

'I couldn't possibly.' But she stares down at the muddy brown coffee in her cup like maybe, just maybe, a little seed has been planted that might begin to sprout.

At school the next day, we each have to spend five minutes with Ms Cartwright going through our 'Plan for Self-Improvement'. When it's my turn, I show her what I've written (now expanded to five pages).

'Wow, Andy,' she says. 'You've clearly given this a lot of thought. I think it's a great idea. Your mum must be over the moon.'

'Yeah.' I glance down at my plan so I don't have to meet her eyes. 'Except I haven't *exactly* told her the whole thing. She loves the shop the way it is. We don't see it in the same way.'

Ms Cartwright taps her long red nail on the page, thinking. 'Take it from me – grown-ups don't always have all the answers.'

'That's for sure,' I mumble.

'Sometimes we have to take risks, do things that other people don't understand, but are for the greater good. Do you understand?'

'Like you did,' I say.

'Like I did. When I was your age, I wasn't brave enough to stand up and be the person I knew I was underneath. That's why I wanted all of you to do this project. To realize that you *can* be brave and take those risks.'

'Right . . .'

'And besides' – she lowers her voice – 'you know I'm one of your mum's customers.'

'Yes.' I blush, recalling the encounter in the shop. 'But I'm a little surprised. You always look so nice.' Today she's wearing a black silk blouse, a short orange velvet skirt, and black faux snakeskin high heels. It all looks really good together.

'Thanks, Andy.' She beams. 'I appreciate you saying that. Your mum sometimes has some hidden gems in her shop, but they can be really hard to find. Hence, from a purely personal point of view, I think you're on the right track. I'm sure that with a few tweaks, you and your mum could make the shop a success again.'

'Thanks, Ms Cartwright,' I say, getting up so

that the next person can have their five minutes. 'You've given me lots to think about.'

I do think about what Ms Cartwright said about being brave and taking risks. I can't imagine what it must have been like for her at my age, knowing that she was in the wrong body, and not knowing what to do about it. My problems may pale in comparison, but they're still important to me. So while I still feel guilty about lying to Mum, I decide that I'm going to continue with my plans. As we go home after school, I tell Stevie and Carrie about Aunt Linda, and how I'm trying to get Mum to go up north so I can get on with the clear-out and the painting at the shop.

'I think you're doing the right thing,' Stevie says. 'And I'm totally up for helping with the painting. I can do the lower down stuff.'

'Great,' I say. 'We'll save that for you.'

'Who's we?' Carrie says. 'I've never painted anything in my life.'

'So – you can start now,' I say. 'It's not that hard.'

'How do you know?'

'Well . . . I've had a little practice, actually.'

I've been dying to tell Stevie and Carrie about the old theatre, and about Thomas. But he told me to keep it a secret so that his uncle didn't find out.

I know my friends won't tell his uncle, so that secret's still safe. But since talking to Ms Cartwright, I've had another Brilliant Idea. Something that will surprise Thomas – be a kind of 'thank you' for letting me sell some of Hélène's clothing. Something that involves Stevie and Carrie. It's funny watching their faces as I tell them exactly what I've been getting up to.

'Jeez, Andy,' Stevie says. 'You mean you've been hanging out with that gorgeous boy from the chippie?'

'Yeah.' I don't smile, but inside I feel a little flash of pride. 'We're like – friends.'

'Friends?' Carrie looks at me in amazement.

'Of course . . .' I suddenly think of the kiss on the cheek, and the dance – even if I did end up in a heap. We may just be friends, but I've never felt anything before like I do when I'm around Thomas.

I guess my face gives me away. 'No way!' Carrie says. 'You guys are like – going out. Is he your boyfriend?'

'No,' I say huffily. 'I'm helping him paint the old theatre, that's all.'

'And his uncle doesn't know what you're doing?' Stevie's eyes widen.

'No. And Mum doesn't know either – about

the shop. I want to keep it that way.'

Carrie shakes her head slowly. 'I think you're bonkers, but I'm happy to help with the painting. It must burn some calories.'

'It's quite hard work to do it right,' I assure her. 'And we'll have to clear the shop out first.'

'So when do we start?' Stevie says.

'Well, there's this little problem of getting Mum to go away for a while. But until that happens, I'm sure Thomas could use a little extra help with the theatre.'

'So . . . ?' Stevie says.

'How about tonight?'

21

A SECRET IS OUT

The three of us meet up again later at Stevie's house and do our homework. Then, instead of watching TV, we tell Stevie's mum that we're going over to Carrie's house. Outside, the sky is steel grey and there's a thin, cloying mist in the air. I hold my school bag over my head to stay dry. Stevie wheels herself along the pavement instead of using the motor, working on strengthening her arms.

When we get to the high street and pass the chippie, I catch a glimpse of Thomas in the back. He's wearing a white apron, and sweat is beading on his forehead as he cooks. Mr LeBoeff is serving a line of customers. I don't wave or call out.

'Come on,' I say to Carrie. 'The entrance is round the back.'

I lead them round to the back alley, but when we get there I'm alarmed to see a light on at the back of Mum's shop. I put a finger to my lips and wave Carrie past quickly. I sneak a glance through the little window in the back door. Mum is inside with piles of clothes around her, writing out more price tags. I feel a sharp pang of guilt. I should be there helping her instead of doing work for someone else. But Mum's made it pretty clear that she doesn't want my help with the shop, and if things are going to change for real, I have to stick to the master plan. Mum's had plenty of chances to make the shop a success but it hasn't happened. I remember what Ms Cartwright said. Just because Mum's a grown-up doesn't mean she has all the answers.

At the back of the old theatre, I get the key from under the mat. I unlock the door — it's just wide enough to squeeze the wheelchair through. Carrie and Stevie start talking and I have to shush them. I don't know how thick the walls are, and I don't want Mum to find us.

When I lead my friends through the curtain to the theatre, both of them gasp — just like I did the first time. 'I had no idea this was here,' Stevie says.

'It's way cool,' Carrie says. 'What are they going to do with it?'

'It's not been decided yet,' I say. 'But one thing's for sure, it will look even better once it's painted. And the ceiling needs two coats.'

'Then we'd better get started,' Stevie says, flexing the muscles of her arms.

My friends get stuck in to the painting, chatting about the old theatre and how often we've walked past it without even wondering what it looked like inside. I try to relax and enjoy what we're doing, but I can't. Mum is on the other side of the wall – how can I get her to take a holiday so I can get on with my plan? And Thomas is next door, slaving away over a hot vat of oil while I've given away his secret. Will he thank me for getting my friends to help out with the painting? Or tell me to get lost?

'Hey, earth to Andy,' I turn around. Stevie is behind me. She's painted a large amount of wall – an even strip from the skirting board to her arm's length. 'I said – when is your boyfriend going to get here?'

I put my hands on my hips. 'I told you, it's not like that.'

'What, he's not coming?' she teases.

'No. The first part.' I turn swiftly back to the wall I'm working on, furiously slathering on paint with the roller.

'Hey, knock it off. I don't need a shower,' Stevie says. I turn around and see that I've accidentally splattered her with tiny white droplets of paint.

'Oh, sorry,' I say drily.

'And stop doing the lower down stuff – you're in my way.' She wheels up to me, and the next thing I know she's painting my back with her brush like I'm a bit of uneven wall.

'Hey!'

Carrie puts down her brush and starts laughing. I grab Stevie's brush out of her hands, dip it in the paint and flick it at her. 'Stop laughing.'

My aim is a little too good. It hits her square in the forehead and begins to drip down her face like she's a statue in a park full of pigeons.

'Oops!' I giggle.

Stevie snorts a laugh.

'That's it – you're toast!' Carrie yells. She runs at me and swipes my face with her brush. I'm laughing so hard that I can't even move quickly.

I swipe back at her with my brush. Stevie grabs the roller and starts painting both of us as we're locked in a fit of giggles. 'This T-shirt was new,'

Carrie says, between gasps of laughter. 'Look what you've done to it!'

'Think of it as a work of art.' I redip my brush and paint a white streak in Stevie's hair. It drips down on to the arm of her wheelchair.

'My chair!' Stevie says. 'Mum's going to go ballistic.'

'Well, you started it!'

We run around chasing each other, flinging paint everywhere. We're laughing so hard that I forget all about Mum and my problems and—

'What are you doing?!?'

22

CAUGHT IN THE ACT!

We all stop dead. Thomas's face is cloudy with anger and disbelief. I hang my head. A drop of paint trickles down my nose. 'Hi,' I mutter, 'we were, um . . .'

'Breaking and entering? Vandalizing this place?' Thomas's voice is icy.

'No,' Stevie says, her voice a squeak. 'We wanted to help.'

Thomas shakes his head.

I look around. Paint is sloshed, flecked and smeared everywhere – and the wheelchair has shifted the drop cloths and left paint streaks all over the wooden floor. Paint cans are turned over, with paint glooping out. Everything is white and sticky-wet — the brush handles, the radio, the packet of biscuits on top of Thomas's toolbox — all our skin, hair and clothing. How could I let this happen — acting like a little kid messing about with my friends? How could I let Thomas down like that? Let myself down?

He turns around and heads back out through the curtain. I hand my brush to Carrie and run to follow him, cringing as paint drips from me and my footprints are white down the corridor.

'Wait, Thomas,' I say. 'Please.'

He goes out the back door. I follow him, closing it behind me. As soon as we're outside, he whirls round to face me. 'Do you think this is funny, Andy?'

'No! I'm sorry! We wanted to help but then things got silly, and—'

'I've been working on this place for months — way before you started "helping" me. Not just the painting but fixing things — the electrics, the plumbing, the heating.'

'I thought I'd surprise you by bringing in extra helpers.' I wince under the chill of his gaze.

'What a great surprise.'

'I'm sorry.' I bite my lip.

'Yeah, well, it doesn't really matter, as it turns out. The estate agent rang me earlier — they've had some interest in the theatre.'

'Some interest?' I frown, not following.

'Someone who wants to buy it. They want to turn it into a gym or a yoga studio – something like that.'

I look at him in dismay. 'But I thought you weren't going to call in the estate agents until the painting was finished.'

'Does it matter? I had someone round a few months ago. Just to get some suggestions. It sounds like they might start revitalizing this end of the high street. So who knows – they might even buy your mum's place too.'

I look at the wall that separates the theatre from the shop. It's true, they used to be joined up . . . it would make sense to knock them through again if someone wanted a larger space. I feel like I've been slapped in the face. 'The *Emporium*? You didn't mention that, did you?' I say, dreading the answer. Thomas lied to me. All my bluster the other day about the ideas and plans I have – well, he must secretly have been laughing.

'I didn't have to. Anyone can see that it's going under.'

'No.' I choke out the word. It strikes me that only a few weeks ago, having someone buy the *Emporium* would have been an answer to my prayers. But not any more. Not when I've built up a new story in my mind and imagined how things could be different – how *I* could make them different. I feel the ground shift under my feet. It's like everything is crumbling to pieces around me. I've been stupid and naive – that much I admit. But Thomas has no right – no right at all – to talk like that about Mum's shop.

I don't realize that I've spoken aloud until I see a cloud pass over Thomas's face.

'Look, I'm sorry,' he snaps back at me. 'But this is a good thing. Your mum sells her shop, my uncle sells the theatre. It's a win–win situation. OK?'

The wet paint on my skin feels like droplets of ice. 'No, it's not OK.' I square my shoulders – I'm at least two inches taller than he is – and stare at him. 'It's not OK because I'm not giving up just like that. *I've* got plans.'

'Good for you.' He shrugs, dismissing me like I'm a silly child. Which is how I've been acting. Then he stalks off. I watch him walk down the alleyway past the last shop. My heart is stretched to breaking point, but I know that I'm right – I just *have* to be.

But it doesn't make it hurt any less.

23

THE WHITE X

All the next day, I feel terrible. I sit in class thinking about how much I've messed up — *again*! After Thomas left, I went back inside the theatre. Carrie and Stevie were already cleaning up. Stevie was zooming around in her chair with a mop, with Carrie on her hands and knees scrubbing any missed spots.

They both looked as glum as I felt. 'Sorry,' the three of us said in unison. Too little, too late.

In the end I didn't tell them what Thomas told me — about the theatre being sold for a gym or a yoga studio. I didn't want to talk about it, or think about it.

Now, as I sit at the back of the class staring at

the clock, I wonder again what it might all mean for *Eliza's Emporium* – that is, if the theatre is sold but Mum keeps her shop. On some level, it might be good to have more people coming past the shop window. But then I have a scary vision of Mum working on a new window display designed to draw in the crowds of yoga-mums and gym-goers: 'Amelie' dressed head-to-toe in second-hand Lycra and trainers. The only thing as bad as old underwear is someone else's sweaty leotards and tights—

'Andy?' Stevie says. I snap back to reality. Class is over and everyone else is filing out of the room. Only Stevie and Carrie have stayed behind. Stevie looks gaunt and tired, her usual energy drained from her face. Behind her, Carrie bites into a fruit and nut bar. She chews it for a few seconds, makes a face like it's disgusting, and spits it out into the wrapper.

'Hi,' I say. 'I'm not feeling very well. I might just go home, OK?'

'We want to meet your friend Thomas properly,' Stevie says firmly. 'We want to say we're sorry.'

'Yeah.' Carrie throws the wrapper in the bin. 'The painting was fun – you know, before we messed everything up.'

'I don't know,' I say. 'I think we've got ourselves into enough trouble. And I'm not sure that Thomas is worth the bother. In fact, the whole thing – my plan . . . well . . .' I trail off, feeling flooded by despair.

Stevie shakes her head. 'Come on, Andy. You're the one who asked *us* to help.'

'So?'

'So, we want to help. For real this time.'

I don't know how I let them talk me into it, but next thing I know, we're all standing around the back door of the old theatre. My stomach feels like I've swallowed a brick. In my mind I know that the theatre will be sold, and probably the shop too. Though I'm still feeling angry and hurt, the truth is that Thomas is right. It's a win–win situation. I sigh. Even if he's wrong, I'd still rather have him as a friend.

The door is propped open with an empty paint can and I can hear the faint sound of the radio. Thomas must be inside. I wish we'd never had the paint fight – I wish I hadn't let Stevie and Carrie in on the secret. I wish I hadn't got angry. But it's way too late for all that now.

'Look,' – I turn to my friends – 'can you give me a minute?'

Stevie and Carrie look at each other, then at

me. 'Sure.' Stevie grins suddenly. 'We wouldn't dream of barging in on the "kiss and make up" bit between you and your *boyfriend*.'

'Stop saying that,' I growl. Hoping that I look braver than I feel, I walk down the corridor to the end and peek through the curtain. I spot the ladder and the paint cans but no Thomas. I go inside.

Thomas is lying down on the stage, his hands beneath his head. At first I think he might be asleep, but then I see that his eyes are open and he's staring up at the ceiling. I walk closer but he doesn't move. 'Thomas?' I say over the sound of the radio that's blaring from next to him.

He reaches out a hand and switches off the radio. 'I didn't think you'd come back,' he says, still not looking at me.

'I'm sorry, Thomas,' I say. 'What my friends and I did was awful. And I . . . I shouldn't have got mad.'

He turns his head towards me, his eyes stormy and hostile.

'I . . . just got caught up in making plans,' I say. 'When we were talking the other night – I had this vision. That this whole place was filled with lovely things – like the polka-dot dress. But it was all just stupid.'

He sits up and slowly gets to his feet. 'It's not stupid,' he says. 'And actually, I'm the one who ought to feel bad. I mean, you've obviously been giving this a lot of thought. Whereas me – well,' he shrugs, 'all I've been doing is painting.'

'No. You've done way more than that. You're trying to help your uncle. Fixing this place up to sell – it makes a lot of sense.' I sigh. 'I wanted to do the right thing too. I thought I could transform the shop, even though I've never done anything like that before. As everyone keeps pointing out, I'm only *thirteen*.'

'What does that have to do with it?' He almost manages a smile.

'I don't know. What I'm trying to say is that if someone wants to buy Mum's shop for a gym and yoga studio, then maybe it's for the best.'

He shakes his head. 'You don't mean that.'

'I don't know what I do or don't mean right now.'

This time he does laugh. 'I get it. I feel exactly the same way. I mean, I've liked fixing this place up. I like being here and imagining what it was like before. Full of people all dressed up, happy and full of life. It's weird, but sometimes when I'm here, I feel this echo of the way it once was – and what it could be again. But now . . .' A shadow crosses his face. 'I don't know either.'

'So why are you here then?'

For a long second he stares at me, and I wonder if he's going to order me to leave once and for all. His eyelashes are long and black as he blinks but doesn't look away. I think about The Kiss and The Dance and my knees suddenly feel like jelly. 'I guess the same reason you are,' he says.

I force myself to breathe. 'OK . . .' I say, 'then I guess we'd better stop sitting around. This place isn't going to paint itself.'

'No, it isn't.' The moment passes, and I feel relieved – but also a tiny bit disappointed. He jumps off the stage and goes over to the stack of paint cans. 'Where are your friends today?' he says. 'We could use the help.'

'We're here.' A voice comes from the direction of the corridor. 'We came to say sorry.'

We both turn to where Stevie and Carrie are peeking their heads through the curtain. A flush creeps over my face – how long have they been there? Thomas gives me a quick glance like he's thinking the same thing. I shrug and wave them inside.

'Meet your new painting crew,' I say.

It's odd how some things – and some people – just seem to click. In this case, it's Thomas and my friends. Luckily . . .

Right on cue, Stevie zooms up in her chair and comes to a stop just centimetres from Thomas's legs. 'Hi, I'm Stevie,' she says. 'Sorry for yesterday.'

'No worries. I'm Thomas.' They shake hands.

Carrie comes up sheepishly behind, gawping at Thomas. In his black T-shirt and jeans, his hair slightly curled around his tanned, olive-skinned face, he looks gorgeous. I feel a ridiculous flash of pride that he's my friend.

'I'm Carrie,' she mutters.

'Nice to meet you, Carrie.' Thomas shakes her limp hand.

'Anyway,' I say, 'we're all sorry for yesterday. But we did do a fair bit of painting before things got . . . um . . . out of control.' I point out to Thomas what we did before our paint fight.

'And we really want to help,' Stevie says. 'Painting is kind of fun. Just leave the low bits to me.' She grins.

Thomas smiles back.

'And it's good exercise,' Carrie adds. 'So much better than boot camp!' When Thomas looks at her questioningly, her cheeks turn bright red.

'What are you going to do with the place when it's done?' Stevie asks.

'Um, I don't really know.' Thomas glances at me. 'It would make a good shop or something like that.'

'Or a good gym and yoga studio,' I counter.

'No! Not that, please!' Carrie says.

'Anyway,' I change the subject, 'whatever it ends up being, it still needs to be painted. So let's get started.'

It takes a few minutes to get everything ready. Carrie helps Thomas spread the drop cloths over the floor, Stevie gets the brushes and rollers, and I pour the paint into trays. Thomas assigns us each to an area and turns the radio back on. As unsettled as things are, I find myself swaying along, brushstrokes in time to the music. It's some kind of eighties revival hour – totally cheesy music, but fun too. Pretty soon, we're all singing along, and chatting and laughing. It's even more fun than a paint fight.

I notice that Thomas keeps glancing over at Stevie as she tries to paint her bit of wall from the wheelchair. She stretches her arm up as far as she can to paint over a rough spot of the wall. When the song comes to an end, she lowers her brush, looking frustrated.

'I wish I could stand up,' she says. 'I want to get at that bit.' She gestures with the brush to a thin crack just out of her reach.

Thomas comes over. At first I think he's going just to paint it for her. Then he sets down his brush, wiping his hands on his jeans. 'Tell me what to do,' he says.

She gives him a surprised smile. 'Lift me here.' She puts her hands on her torso just above her waist.

Thomas lifts her up. Stevie stretches up and paints over the crack. Both Carrie and I stop and watch.

'OK, you can lower me down now,' Stevie says.

'OK,' Thomas puffs. Because Stevie's lower half is mostly dead weight, I can tell that lifting her is a bit of an effort.

She settles back in her chair and twists from side to side, stretching. 'I'm learning to walk,' she tells Thomas. 'Some day I'll be rollering along with the best of them.'

'Cool,' Thomas says.

'But for now,' Stevie says, 'maybe I should get us something to drink.'

'There's a fridge at the back with some Cokes,' Thomas says.

'I'll come with you,' Carrie says to Stevie. I pretend not to see the wink she gives me. They go off towards the little kitchen in the back corridor.

Without a word, Thomas comes up beside me. 'Thank you, Andy,' he says. As he traces an x on my cheek with white paint, my insides quietly melt.

24

OPERATION MUM HOLIDAY

'I'm really not happy, Andy.' Aunt Linda tsks like I'm a spoiled child. 'You shouldn't have made your mum more worried.'

'I know, and I'm really sorry. But I know it's for the best.'

It's the day after I made up with Thomas and my friends helped with the painting. I can still feel the phantom outline of the x on my cheek. Every time I think about it, I start to feel all funny and flushed. But I can't worry about whether there might or might not be something between me and Thomas. I can't even worry about what's going to happen to the old theatre. Right now, I need to keep focused on *my* plan.

Aunt Linda sighs. 'Of course I'd love to see Eliza. It's been so long. And Mother's arthritis *is* getting worse. But I'm not going to lie to her.'

'I know – and I'm not asking you to. It's just that she won't go unless she thinks that *you* need *her*.'

'So now you're a psychologist?'

'No!' I say. 'I just want her to get better. And I don't think she can do that here – where all this . . . stuff . . . is going wrong with the shop.'

Aunt Linda is silent for a moment. I cross my fingers.

'OK, I'll do it. I will ask her to come up here.'

Result!

'Thanks, Aunt Linda,' I say. 'It's the right thing.'

'Hmmf.'

'Bye for now. Love you.' I hang up the phone, a big grin on my face. Part One of the plan is now one step closer.

That night, I begin to wonder if maybe Part One of the plan is working a little *too* well. Mum comes into my room, her eyes puffy and red-rimmed, like she's been crying.

'What's the matter?' I say, my heart seizing up.

'Your Aunt Linda rang.' Her mouth twitches as she tries to make herself smile. 'My mum isn't well – she's frail . . . in pain. I haven't seen my family in such a long time. It's terrible . . .'

'You should definitely go up there,' I say.

Maybe I sound a little too eager, because for a second Mum's eyes narrow. Then she moves away and looks at my shelf. She picks up a trophy I won for a swimming race a long time ago and turns it over in her hands.

'I don't know . . .' she falters. She sets down the trophy and stares out the window into the darkness. Some stuff I read on the internet about depression pops into my mind:

Difficulty in making decisions . . .

'I think it would be good for you to see your mum and your sister,' I say. 'Get away for a little bit.'

She sighs. 'It's just not a good time right now. I'm so tired. It's such a lot of effort . . .'

Difficulty in taking action . . .

She walks over to my bed and sinks down on it. 'Besides, you've got school.'

'I'm fine staying with Stevie. It will be good.' I take a breath. 'Maybe we both need some time apart.'

'You mean you want rid of me – your old sadsack Mum.'

Internal dialogue of self-blame . . .

I grab her hand. 'No, Mum – that's not it at all. I just think that maybe you need a break, and I'm fine staying here because I've got school. I can totally focus on that. It's a no-brainer.'

'I don't know . . .'

Constant second-guessing . . .

'Go, Mum. See your mum and your sister. Take long walks in the hills. Breathe in the fresh air of the Lakes. Clear your head. I'll be fine.'

'But the shop . . . ?'

Placement of obstacles . . .

'It isn't going anywhere.'

'Well . . .' She hesitates. 'Actually, there's something I should tell you. It may be the answer to our prayers.' Her mouth sets in a straight line.

'What?' My stomach dips.

'An estate agent called me the other day. Someone is interested in the old theatre. They want to turn it into a gym or something.'

'Oh—?'

'He thinks I might be able to sell up. They can use the floor space. Apparently there's some big push to revitalize our end of the high street.'

'But Mum, you can't!' I say.

'The shop is failing, Andy.' A tear forms in the corner of her eye.

'But if it wasn't, you'd keep it, right?'

'I love my shop. You know that. It's been everything to me – other than you, of course.' She wipes her eye with her sleeve. 'But I can't pass up this opportunity. It would be wrong of me – and you deserve better. We could start again somewhere else. Some day . . .'

'But this is our home. There is nowhere else. Don't do it for me – I'm fine.'

She throws up her hands. 'Look, I don't know. It will probably all come to nothing. I think you're right, though – I do need to get away. Think things through.'

'It really is the best thing,' I say, trying to reassure her. 'You need time. If the gym people really want it, then they'll wait. You have to make the right decision – for . . . us.'

'Yes, you're right. I don't want to make the wrong decision.'

I edge closer and lean my head on her shoulder. 'So when will you go?'

'I'll need to talk to Stevie's mum. And take care of a few things at the shop. But if I can get that done, then . . . I don't know . . . maybe on Monday?'

'OK, Mum.' I turn and put my arms around her, holding her tight. Now that she's going – the one thing I need in order to get started with my plans – I really do feel like crying. 'I'll miss you lots, but take all the time you need.'

25

GLAD RAGS AND BIN BAGS

After school on Monday, I give Mum a kiss through the window of the minicab that will take her to the train station. I feel a sharp ache inside like a part of me has been torn off – Mum and I have always been together, and now she's going away. I'm going to miss her so much. But she'll be back, and while she's gone I have a job to do.

As soon as the taxi disappears around the bend at the end of the road, I go back inside the house to get the spare key. I've arranged to meet Stevie and Carrie after dinner at *Eliza's Emporium*, and we're going to go through everything in the shop and give it either the thumbs up, or the thumbs out. I've already bought two rolls of black plastic bin bags. Rubbish collection day is tomorrow, so there's not much time.

But I soon discover there's a problem – no key in the drawer. 'No!' I yell. Who knew that Mum would suddenly go all security-conscious now that she's going on holiday? I ransack the kitchen and Mum's sewing room, but there's nothing. I feel like screaming as I walk to the shop to meet my friends.

Stevie and Carrie are waiting for me around the back.

'What's the matter?' Stevie says as soon as she sees my face.

'We have a problem,' I say. 'No key. Either Mum's hidden the spare one or she took it with her. I can't find it anywhere.'

I kick at the mat outside the door, hoping that Mum will have gone back to her old ways. But there's no key there either. I scan the back of the shop. There are no windows other than a tiny one at the top of the door. Other than breaking through the front of the shop – obviously not an option – there's no way in. Despair floods through me. This is my big chance. I can't let it come to nothing.

'What about your *boyfriend*?' Stevie gestures

down the alleyway towards the theatre, and beyond that the chippie. 'Maybe he can pick the lock.'

'Don't call him that,' I grumble.

Seeing as there's no other choice, I go off down the alley. The theatre door is closed, but the back door to the chippie is open.

I've never gone down the alley as far as the chippie before. I can hear the sound of a radio; smell the fish frying in the vats. It's also a few degrees hotter the closer I get. I go up to the door and take a quick peek inside, half hoping that Thomas isn't there. But I see him – the back of him anyway, as he's chopping potatoes. His dark hair is slicked back, and he's wearing a white apron. He looks kind of rough and edgy – as good as someone can working in a chip shop.

'Psst, Thomas,' I whisper loudly. He keeps chopping and doesn't turn around.

'Thomas,' I say, louder this time.

He gives a little start like I've pulled him out of his own world. He turns around. 'Oh, it's you.' Setting down the knife, he comes over to the door, wiping his forehead on the apron. He seems a little embarrassed.

'Sorry to bother you at work.'

He laughs. 'Um, don't be.'

'It's just, we've got a problem. Mum's shop is locked. I think she took the key with her.'

'Did you look for another key?'

'Yeah, I couldn't find one.'

'OK, did you try breaking in?' He doesn't miss a beat.

'How? We can't do it through the front. The window in the back door is too small.'

'Thomas?' Mr LeBoeff calls from the front counter. 'I need those potatoes in now. And two scampis.'

I clench my teeth. 'Sorry,' I say. 'I can see this isn't a good time.'

'No,' he says. 'But give me half an hour.'

In fact, it's only twenty minutes later that I slump down in the middle of the parquet floor of the theatre, guilt stinging in my chest. 'We can't!' I look at Carrie and Stevie. Why don't they see that Thomas's 'idea' for getting into Mum's shop is a complete non-starter. I never should have asked for his help.

'Well . . .' Stevie stares at the blank white wall, cocking her head. 'I don't see another option right this second. And if Thomas is willing . . .'

Thomas looks more than willing. He hefts the sledgehammer over his shoulder like he's God's gift to construction work. Or in this case, demolition. His plan for getting into Mum's shop is to knock down part of the wall between the theatre and *Eliza's Emporium*.

Carrie's mouth keeps gaping open when she looks at Thomas. 'It's not going to bring the whole place down, is it?' she asks.

'No,' he says. 'The shop used to be part of the theatre. The partition was put up later. It's not structural.'

'What's on the other side of the wall?' Stevie asks me.

I picture the inside of Mum's shop. On the long wall she has the rack of old jeans and some shelves with handbags, the wedding dresses and the torso of the mannequin wearing the coconut bra and Hawaiian skirt . . .

'Actually . . .' I say with a long sigh. 'Go ahead.'

Thomas gleefully hefts the hammer. Even with my hands over my ears, there's an almighty *THUD* as the hammer hits the wall. Nothing happens. I don't know if I'm disappointed, or secretly glad.

'Whew, OK.' Thomas flexes his hands.

He raises the hammer and swings again. The wall seems to judder a little, but that's it.

'Maybe over a little more,' Thomas puffs. 'Got to find a weak spot.'

'The wall should be weakest right in the middle,' Stevie says. 'If a doorway was filled in like you say, it will be stronger near the edges where the support is.'

'OK, Einstein.' Thomas grins at her. I feel a pesky little buzz of jealousy, but I ignore it. I'm glad that Thomas and my friends are getting along so well.

He moves over another metre and swings the hammer. This time, instead of a thud, there's a distinct *CRACK!*

'One more and you're there,' Stevie says. 'Stand back, everyone.' She whizzes her chair backwards. Carrie and I join her near the centre of the room.

'Arrraugh,' Thomas cries. He swings. There's another *crack!* Suddenly there's dust and rubble everywhere, and a hammer-sized hole in the middle of the wall.

'Stand back, Thomas,' Stevie cries.

Thomas ignores her and gets ready to swing the hammer again. But before he can do so, there's another cracking sound. The bricks seem to hover, suspended in slow motion. Then, three metres of wall begin to crumble to the floor.

'Yeah!' Thomas yells. He jumps back.

Even standing back, the dust is so thick that it covers us. Carrie begins to cough. Thomas's black hair is covered in dust. It's like we've all been in a snowstorm or a sandstorm. But we're through. Thomas turns to me, laughing. I must look a sight. The next thing I know, we're hugging each other.

I'm still there when the dust begins to clear. Behind me, I hear giggling and little kissy noises. I pull away from Thomas. If my face wasn't white with dust, it would be bright red.

I turn back to my friends. 'What are you looking at?' I glare. I walk forward to where the dust has settled. In the midst of the white-painted bricks and rubble, I see a broken mannequin with a rubble-covered coconut bra and a Hawaiian grass skirt. I see a few pairs of dust-covered jeans peeking out from beneath the bricks, and at the front of the shop 'Amelie' standing at the window looking out, her black dress now polka-dotted with dust.

And a slow, warm feeling begins to creep over me. I go over to my bag and take out the twenty-pack of black bin liners I bought. Thanks to the lack of a key, suddenly everything just got easier.

26

NIGHT FEVER

We're all so dirty that it seems best just to get stuck in. The four of us get on with clearing the bricks and rubble. Carrie and I load the bricks into old paint buckets, and Stevie whizzes them in her wheelchair out the back of the theatre where Thomas helps her dump them into the big steel skip behind the chippie. But it takes a long time even to make a small dent in what we need to move. All in all, about five metres of wall ended up coming down – all of which had been filled in beneath an old arch between the theatre and the shop. Five metres of Mum's stock on racks that are now completely buried like a junk shop in Pompeii.

Such a shame, I think with a glow of satisfaction.

It takes trip after trip and I start to think that we're never going to finish moving the bricks let alone anything else. Finally, we get to the point where I start picking up the rubble-strewn clothes. I shake the dust off them and start stuffing them into the bin bags.

'What if your mum wants some of them?' Carrie says.

'The whole point is that what she doesn't see won't hurt her,' Stevie says.

I pick up the mannequin with the coconut bra. She's so old and cheesy that she doesn't even have real fake hair – it's painted on. Since falling down off the high shelf, she's now missing an arm.

'*Au revoir.*' I shove her torso into the bag, grass skirt, plastic lei and all. The arm sticks out of the top of the bag. 'Here.' I pile the thing on to Stevie's lap. 'Give her a proper burial.' Stevie whizzes her off in her wheelchair.

Carrie and I shake the dust off some of the wedding dresses. 'I just can't believe people give away their wedding dresses,' I say, frowning at the yellow sweat stains under the arms of one of the dresses – satin with a poufy skirt and a row of seed pearl buttons down the back. I wonder who wore it, and if she looked nice on her special day. It's kind of sad that I'll never know.

'I guess they keep them for ever, and then die. No one wants them any more.'

I put the dress down, shuddering. Carrie's right. Most of the wedding dresses probably did come from the estates of people who died.

'That one's stained, but this one's kind of nice.' Carrie holds up a dress in ivory silk with tiny crystals sewn in a pattern of flowers and swirls on the bodice. She checks the tag. 'Maggie Sottero,' she says. 'I think I've heard of that brand. Your mum was selling it for ten pounds.'

I frown. Like Ms Cartwright said, maybe it's possible that Mum's shop does have a few hidden gems – being sold way too cheap. 'Put it to one side,' I say. 'We'll have to look at each—'

Before I can finish the sentence, I hear a shout of laughter coming from the theatre.

I look up and across the vast expanse of floor. Stevie's come back in after her trip to the skip. She's got the radio in her lap and switches it on, then holds the velvet curtain aside.

Thomas struts in. He's wearing the coconut bra over his T-shirt, the grass skirt over his jeans, and a pair of old jeans tied over his head like a turban. He walks forward towards us, all the way across the theatre, shaking his hips like a hula dancer. I look at Carrie; she looks at me. We both bust up laughing. He shakes his shoulders, does a little turn, then a pose.

'Here, Kate Moss, try this.' Carrie tosses him the stained wedding dress. He slips it over his head, goes over to the window where 'Amelie' is standing oblivious. He grabs her and whirls her around. He gives her a big kiss on her painted mouth, then trips on the hem of the dress and they collapse to the floor on top of the rubble. I'm laughing so hard that tears come to my eyes.

'Jeez, Andy, she's a worse dancer than you are,' Thomas says, wiping the dust off himself.

'Thanks,' I say. 'But maybe it's your lead.' I hold out my hand and pull him up out of the rubble.

'Maybe.' Laughing, he picks up 'Amelie' and puts her back in her window.

Stevie and Carrie take up the game. Carrie tries on a puffy gold prom dress that makes her look like a Christmas bauble. Stevie finds the rack of hats and tries them on one by one – a policeman's hat, a little round pillbox hat with a red veil, an American football helmet.

'Go, Patriots.' Thomas knocks on the helmet.

I spy something on one of the racks – it's totally outrageous, but I have to try it on.

'No peeking,' I say. I take it to the back and get

changed. It takes a little time – the trousers are tight, even on me. When I go back out to the main part of the shop, though, it's totally worth it.

'Oh . . . my . . .' Carrie's mouth drops open.

'Brilliant!' Stevie giggles.

Thomas comes up to me, the wedding dress still hanging off him. He takes my arm and positions me in front of the mirror.

I can't even believe that I'm wearing these clothes – an orange crushed-velvet suit from the seventies with huge bell-bottom trousers and platform shoes. My skin and hair are covered with dust – I look like some kind of creature from a scary rock video. Scary, but kind of cool too. Stevie changes the station on the radio and finds some electronic disco music. The song ends and another one comes on: 'Night Fever'.

'Come on, let's dance!' I grab Carrie by the hand. Laughing, she tries to spin me under her arm, and I have to duck down about a foot. Stevie rocks her wheelchair to the music and Thomas does his funny hip-shaking thing again. I'm laughing and sweating, and it's so much fun that I wish we could be here, in this strange little world between the old theatre and the wreck of Mum's shop, for ever.

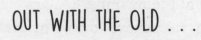

27

OUT WITH THE OLD . . .

The song ends. Eventually we stop dancing, stop laughing, and gradually come to our senses. Mum's shop is a wreck; there's so much to do. I change wistfully out of the orange velvet suit, and the others take off their bits and pieces.

I shove the stained wedding dress into a bin bag, and put the Maggie Sottero dress and the orange velvet suit to one side. I can see that it's going to be harder than I thought to go through everything, because some things might be worth keeping.

Carrie and Stevie get on with going through some of the clothes, and Thomas checks out the racks that have fallen down. 'We can use these,' he says to me. 'Maybe not for the front of the shop, but for the back.'

'Can't we just get rid of it all?' I say. 'Start again?'

'Shop fittings cost money,' Thomas says. 'You should keep what you can.'

'OK. You're probably right,' I say.

I walk over to the edge of the arch. Through the knocked-down wall, the theatre is like a big white blank canvas. The arch is elegant with little bunches of plaster fruit that just need another coat of white paint. Having the two spaces together seems right somehow. Like they've been finally reunited. Will they become a gym and yoga studio, or a fabulous shop? Or something completely different? Right now, I don't have a clue.

'It's such a classic building.' Thomas says, coming up beside me like he's reading my thoughts. 'It would be a shame to turn it into a gym.'

'A gym?' Stevie says. She swivels her chair and comes towards me. 'So you were serious when you said that?'

'Someone is interested in buying the theatre and the shop,' Thomas says. 'Their idea was to turn it into a gym and yoga studio.'

Stevie frowns at me. 'I thought this was about redoing the *Emporium* for your mum.'

'For me it is.' I don't look at Thomas.

There's an uncomfortable silence.

'Sorry,' Stevie says. 'I'm getting a little confused here. Do we need to go outside until you two sort it out?'

'No!' Thomas and I say at the same time.

'O . . . K,' Stevie says. 'Um, do you want to tell us what's going on?'

I plunk down on the floor. Thomas paces back and forth.

'I first had the idea to transform Mum's shop when I discovered Thomas working on the theatre – just on the other side of the wall,' I say.

'My uncle owns the theatre,' Thomas clarifies.

'So what was he planning on doing with it?' Carrie asks, looking shyly at Thomas.

'It's a long story,' Thomas says. 'The point is that it's been sitting here empty all these years. I thought that if he sold the theatre he could move back to Paris.'

'Makes sense, I guess,' Stevie says. 'Does your uncle want that too?'

'Not exactly,' Thomas admits. 'I've kind of been keeping the whole thing a secret from him. I wanted to surprise him by fixing the place up and showing him that it was possible. My uncle has lots of friends and family back in Paris. I know he's torn – he feels sentimental about staying here, but Paris is his home.'

'Gosh,' Carrie says. 'It's kind of a mess, then.'

'Kind of.' Thomas nods. 'I know I need to talk to him soon. Really soon, in fact.'

'Yeah.' Stevie frowns. 'You do.'

He sighs. 'Everything seemed really clear to me. But then when Andy told me her whole idea, I wasn't so sure. I've given it some thought, and I think her idea is really good. Have you told them?' He turns to me.

'Not the whole thing.'

'Tell them.'

As I begin to talk, I wonder if he's torturing me. Describing my 'vision' in front of Stevie's logical scrutiny and Carrie's down-to-earth common sense is hard – harder than when it was just me and Thomas, brainstorming and thinking aloud. As I speak, all the problems swirl around in my head. How to get good stock and new customers, how to come up with a new brand and *relaunch* the business. Even if I could get my head around all that, at the end of the day, I'm *only thirteen*.

'Wow,' Stevie says when I've finally finished my

spiel. 'That's quite . . . um . . . ambitious.'

'I think it's awesome,' Carrie says. 'It's a brilliant idea to combine your mum's shop and the theatre back into one. You have to do it.'

Thomas pushes his dark hair back from his face. 'It's totally crazy,' he says. 'But that's what's cool about it.'

I look around me and all I can see is the rubble and debris of the knocked-down wall. A great big mess. When I had my original idea to transform Mum's shop, there wasn't anyone out there wanting to buy the shop to turn it into something else. But now I realize how much is riding on my plans – Mum's future, Mr LeBoeff's, Thomas's, mine – and I suddenly feel overwhelmed. I shake my head slowly and look at Stevie. 'No,' I say, 'you're right. It *is* too ambitious. I have no business thinking I can do this . . . this enormous project all on my own.'

'But you're not on your own,' Carrie says. 'You've got us.'

Thomas eyes me critically. 'It's going to take a lot of guts and nerve, but I thought you had that.'

'I don't know. I just want my mum to be happy. But she's not even here. I'm keeping more secrets from her – and I didn't want to do that.'

'It's for her own good,' Stevie says.

Thomas steps forward, shaking his head. 'Look, Andy, you have to decide.' I can tell that he's annoyed by my lack of courage. 'You convinced me that your idea could work, but if you're chickening out, then that's that, I guess.' He turns and walks towards the back of the theatre. 'I'm going now to help my uncle close up. You guys lock the door on your way out.' He tosses me the keys.

As soon as he's gone, it's like the air from the room has deflated like a balloon.

'Is there any reason you can't do both?' Carrie says. 'I mean, fix up the shop but also talk to the gym people. Property doesn't just get sold overnight, you know.'

I don't know, but it sounds like she does.

'My dad's got some rental flats,' she adds. 'He's bought and sold lots of properties. It always seems to take ages.'

'I'm sure you're right,' I say. 'And it's so great that you're on board. It's just . . . I don't want to waste everyone's time.' I look at Stevie. 'You believe in parallel universes and wormholes and things. Can't you see into the future and see what I'm supposed to do – get the shop ready for Mum to sell, or fix it up?'

'I wish I could,' Stevie says, 'but the thing is, you had a plan. Why not stick to it and see what happens? Ms Cartwright's right about one thing: that sometimes we need to be a little braver. You've started this, and now the only thing that's stopping you is you.'

'You do sound like Ms Cartwright!' I can't help but laugh a little.

Stevie smiles too. 'Come on, Andy. This is your chance. You may as well have a go.'

'Yeah,' Carrie says. 'We'll finish sorting through the stock. And once that's done, we can start painting.'

'Bring lots of crisps,' Stevie says.

'Yeah, and maybe we can order pizza.'

'Sounds like a plan,' Carrie says.

'Yeah,' I say, smiling. 'It does.'

28

IN WITH THE NEW?

I feel much better knowing that my friends are on board, and so enthusiastic about the plan. But that night, lying on the sofa bed in Stevie's spare room, I can't sleep. Doubts creep back into my mind. How am I going to get the shop fitted out by the time Mum comes back, especially since now it's missing half the main wall? How am I going to get new things to sell – nice things? And then there's Thomas. I'm happy for Stevie and Carrie's help – and I'm really going to need it – but I miss the time we spent just the two of us doing up the old theatre. And it's confusing the way he seems to blow hot and cold. One minute he wants to sell the theatre, and the next he's disappointed in me for being a coward. But either way, I need to talk to him.

After school, Stevie, Carrie and I go directly to the shop to do some sorting of stock before dinner. As we still don't have a key to the shop, we let ourselves in through the old theatre. When I see the knocked-down wall, I feel the knots tighten in my stomach. What started as a make-over of a shop has now become a huge project! But the only way forward is to stick to the plan.

'Start going through the stuff in the back,' I instruct them.

'OK ...' Stevie says. 'But what about you?'

'I've got an errand I need to run.'

Stevie raises an eyebrow. She mouths the word: 'Boyfriend?'

I roll my eyes. 'I'll be back in half an hour. If not, I'll see you at your house later. OK?'

I walk down the alley to the back of the chippie and stick my head in the back door. But Thomas isn't there. Instead, I find myself face to face with Mr LeBoeff.

'Oh, hi,' I say, embarrassed. 'I was um ...'

'Andrea.' He puts down the knife he's using to chop up some fish into goujons. 'I haven't seen you for a while.'

'Yeah, I guess not. Things have been kind of hectic.'

'And how is your mother?' He goes to the sink and washes his hands.

'She's up north visiting her mum and sister,' I say. 'She's taking a break – from the shop and stuff.'

Mr LeBoeff nods. 'Good,' he says. 'A holiday sounds sensible. You know I was worried about her.'

'Yeah. Thanks for that. I think it will be good for her.'

He smiles faintly, and begins wiping down the work surface with a cloth. Since Thomas isn't here, I should just go. But I don't. Thomas said he was going to talk to his uncle about the theatre. I don't know if he's done it yet, and I don't want to betray a confidence. But now that I'm here, I realize that this is the thing that's holding me back. Thomas and I can't do this all on our own – eventually, his uncle is going to need to know. His future is on the line too. Before I can talk myself out of it, I speak up. 'Um, Mr LeBoeff, I was wondering . . . about the old theatre.'

He stops what he's doing. 'The theatre?'

'Thomas says it belongs to you. That you bought it for your wife. Before she . . . died. I wondered if you had any plans for it.'

'Thomas told you, did he?' He grins. 'And here I thought you stopped by to brighten my day with a chat.'

'Oh. Sorry.'

'No matter. You are both young. It is natural to be drawn together.'

'It's not like that,' I say. Maybe it's the hot vats of oil, but I suddenly feel myself breaking out in a sweat. 'We're just friends.'

'Friends . . .' His mouth creases. After a moment, he nods. 'I think that is for the best.'

I raise an eyebrow. I hate to admit it, but his comment really stings. Does he think I'm not good enough for his nephew or something? Not that Thomas would ever want me as a girlfriend – or that I'd even want to be his girlfriend. It's just that sometimes – like when he kissed me on the cheek, and drew the white x – I think about what it might be like if I was.

Mr LeBoeff rinses the cloth in the sink. 'You see, lately I have become worried about the boy.'

'Worried? About Thomas? Why?'

He shakes his head. 'He does not talk to me. He does not come home. He is doing something in secret. I worry that he has fallen in with . . . what do you say? . . . a bad crowd.'

'A bad crowd?' I choke back a laugh.

'I do not know what they get up to. And so far his schoolwork has not suffered. But is he drinking? What is he doing? He is only fourteen years old. Perhaps, Andrea, you can reassure me on this point.' His face is so earnest, so full of love and concern, that I can't just let him go on thinking the worst.

'I don't know who he hangs out with at his school, but as far as I know, he's not doing anything bad after school. Quite the opposite. He's very, um . . . focused.'

Mr LeBoeff leans against the work surface like a great load has settled on him.

'It is difficult, you know, this business of raising a child. Thomas has a great future ahead of him – I believe that with all my heart. He is intelligent and, as you say, focused. But sometimes I worry that he does not believe in himself. That being here – working here' – he sweeps his hands around him – 'he feels that there is nothing out there for him that's better than this.'

'Maybe . . .' I think about what he's saying. For a few years now I've felt trapped – by Mum's shop and my stupid hang-up about the clothes. My new project has given me a purpose – a new way of looking at things. And Thomas has a goal too – helping out his uncle. A goal that he hasn't communicated to him.

'At least Thomas thinks about his future,' I say. 'That's a lot more than I can say.'

Mr LeBoeff nods. 'Yes, he does.' He turns to go back to work. I realize that I've let the conversation stray off topic.

'Mr LeBoeff, about the theatre?' I say. 'What are you planning to do with it?'

He studies me. 'Why do I have to "do" anything with it?'

'It's just that I've heard that there's a developer who wants to open up a gym around here. You could sell up. Move back to Paris.'

'Paris?' He looks a bit stunned.

I realize that I'm on the cusp of giving away a major confidence here. Thomas said he would talk to his uncle, but he clearly hasn't done it yet. In a split second I weigh up the options. Thomas is doing what he's doing for his uncle's own good – same as I'm doing for Mum. And right now, I think it's in everyone's best interest to get things out in the open.

'I know it's none of my business.' I take a breath, stumbling on. 'And believe me, it only started out because I was worried about my mum. I think you might already know – or have suspected – that she's been feeling really low. It's because the shop is failing. I wanted to do something to help her save it. I wanted to change it into something that sells more than just old junk.'

He smiles warily. 'It is a very good thing, Andrea, that you are helping your mum. But what does that have to do with the theatre – and a gym? And . . .' his eyebrows rise, 'Paris?'

'Thomas wanted to help you too,' I stumble on. 'He thought he could fix up the theatre so you could sell it.'

'And why would I want to sell it?'

I swallow hard. 'So you could move back to Paris. He thinks you'd be happier. He was doing it for your own good.'

'So that's what he's been up to.' His face softens with relief.

'I was helping him paint the theatre. He was going to get it valued – see what it was worth. But the estate agent says someone is interested in turning it into a gym – along with Mum's shop.' I take a breath. 'But I've had another idea. It's kind of far-fetched, but it's like . . . I don't know . . . my vision. An amazing high-end fashion shop. Like a *dépôt-vente*.' The word sounds silly coming out of my mouth. 'It's a crazy idea, really. I mean, I'm thirteen years old. I'm sure it sounds totally stupid.'

'Show me what you've done,' he says, taking off his apron and putting it on a peg.

'What? You mean now?' My mind races for an excuse. I can't let him go in there. Half-painted, with a knocked-down wall—

'Yes, I want to see.'

'Thomas is going to kill me . . . !'

Mr LeBoeff takes a ring of keys off a peg next to the door.

'Show me.'

29

DREAMS — OLD AND NEW

ike a prisoner marching to the gallows, I lead
the way to the back door of the theatre. Mr
LeBoeff doesn't even have to bother with the
key — I'm pretty sure Stevie and Carrie are still
inside sorting stock at the back of Mum's shop,
and the door is already unlocked. I pray that
Thomas isn't inside — that he doesn't see me
bringing his uncle in. I know I'm doing it for
Thomas's own good, but he's bound not to see it
that way. Maybe somehow, if I can avoid him, he'll
just think that Mr LeBoeff went in on his own.
The phantom x burns on my cheek — and it seems
a long time ago. Maybe we'll never be more than
just friends, but the idea of Thomas hating me is

just too awful to think about.

Mr LeBoeff goes inside. I follow as he walks slowly down the corridor, looking around like he hasn't been in there for a long time. When he gets to the curtain, he rubs his fingers over the velvet nap, like he's struggling with his memories. I hold my breath until he finally pushes it aside and goes through.

I stand beside him as he gasps and crosses himself, muttering softly. I want to speak – to explain – but for once I keep quiet. He walks around, craning his neck at the ceiling, at the columns, at the pure white walls. His gaze skims over the smashed wall and the half-ransacked inside of Mum's shop. I can hear the faint sound of Carrie and Stevie talking at the back of the shop. Mr LeBoeff doesn't seem to notice. He walks around and around, lost in thought, all the while talking under his breath. To himself – or maybe, to someone else. His wife – Hélène. The person who the theatre was meant for. Finally, he stops walking. He stands right in the centre, his back to me. I'm tempted to sneak out – surely he must have forgotten that I'm even here. But then he speaks.

'Thomas didn't know her,' he says, half to himself. 'Not the way she was ... before.'

'I'm sorry,' I whisper.

'I've never told him the truth. How Hélène fell apart – with her illness, and about when his parents died. It just seemed too difficult to explain.'

'Does he remember his parents?' I say.

'Not really. He was very young at the time. I suppose that is a blessing. And Hélène too has been gone for many years. I just wish' – his eyes fill with tears – 'that she was here to see this.'

'If she had lived, what would you have done here?'

He gives me a kindly smile. 'We had a grand plan together. A plan that was worthy of her past, and mine.' His eyes glaze over with memory. 'Once, the name Pierre LeBoeff meant something in Paris.'

'What was it like there?' I say.

'It was a different world,' he says. 'I owned a café in *Saint Germain-des-Prés* on the Left Bank. And Hélène was more than just a model – she was a muse. For some of the greatest designers of her time. Christian Lacroix, Guy Paulin, Thierry Mugler, Angelo Tarlazzi, Jean Paul Gaultier . . . they called her "La Belle Hélène".'

'The Beautiful Hélène,' I say.

'But she started to become ill, and then her brother's death – it all came very suddenly. I knew we had to get away – start again. A new life. We found the old theatre, and she had an idea to start a fashion school. A place to foster the next generation of designers. She had bad days – days when she had trouble believing in her dream. But mostly the theatre gave her hope. Hope for the future.'

'Thomas told me about the school,' I say. 'I mean, it sounds great and all. But it would be really difficult to open a school.'

He nods. 'You are right. It would have been very difficult. But I was not afraid of that. I would have done anything to make the vision real for her. Unfortunately, the cancer had other plans.'

He takes out a handkerchief and dabs a tear from his eye. Instead of turning away embarrassed, I put my hand on his arm to comfort him.

'She sounds like a very special person,' I say.

'Special, yes.' His eyes glitter. He puts his hand on mine and squeezes it. Then he takes a step away, still looking around him with awe.

'But you never went through with the plan.'

'No. I couldn't. In that way she was right. I couldn't do it – after she was gone. And yet, Andrea, so many times, I wish I had done so. It would have been a testament to her – to her memory. I suppose that's why I kept it all these years – I was being sentimental. But Thomas is right. I have thought from time to time about moving back to Paris. Maybe it would have been for the best.'

'I understand.'

And I do understand, in a way, at least. But now that he's here, I feel like there's an elephant in the room sitting on my chest and squashing me. What now? What next?

He turns back to me and I realize that I've voiced my questions aloud.

'Andrea,' he says, 'I do not know what the future holds. For me, there are reasons to leave, but perhaps' – he pauses for a long time, then suddenly looks in the direction of Mum's shop – 'there are also reasons to stay. But what I do know is that you and Thomas have transformed this place. It is exactly what I once pictured in my mind.'

'It is? You mean . . .' I let out a pent-up breath. 'You're not mad at us?'

He smiles sadly. 'You and Thomas are young, as Hélène and I were once. Tell me more about this "vision" of yours.'

So I do.

It's weird, I think, as I stand alone in the centre of the theatre an hour later. Weird how the universe has a way of making what's supposed to happen happen, even if it seems impossible. Stevie would probably have some kind of scientific explanation for it — string theory or the Higgs Boson or wrinkles in the time-space continuum or something — but right now, it's just kind of doing my head in. In a good way . . . for once.

Mr LeBoeff listened. He didn't talk, he just let me talk. That was pretty weird — also in a good way. I didn't feel like I was thirteen, just like I was a person with an idea, and the energy to make it work. I found myself telling him about my newest idea — one that I haven't even shared with my friends or Thomas.

The idea is that we could turn the dressing rooms into studios that design students from the college could use. They could sell their designs in the shop rather than on a market stall — it would all be very cutting edge. The shop would have consignment, vintage, new designer fashion, and I even voice aloud another thought I had — about turning Mum's shop back into a café and fashion bookstore. The shop would become a place where people would want to come from all over to visit. We don't need a gym and a yoga studio to transform this end of the high street. We can do it ourselves.

Mr LeBoeff had wandered around the vast space, not speaking. But when he'd turned back to me, his eyes were bright.

'Come with me.' He'd gestured for me to follow him.

And once again I'd found myself following a member of the LeBoeff family backstage in the old theatre. He unlatched a small door that I hadn't noticed before. Instead of leading to a dressing room, it led to a set of stairs going down into blackness.

He flipped a switch and a bare bulb lit up at the bottom of the stairs. I followed him down the narrow, rickety staircase. And when I reached the bottom, it was my turn to gasp . . .

At first I imagined that I'd stumbled on some kind of weird Madame Tussauds chamber of horrors or something. But upon a second look, I saw that the vast space was full of mannequins – headless white torsos without arms or legs, each with a number stamped on it to indicate the size.

The rest of the room was full of chrome racks, long tables, chairs, stage lights, and bits of old scenery and props. One corner of the room held a muddled mass of cables and electrical wires, looking like coiled snakes in the dim, flickering light.

'Where are we?' I asked.

'Under the stage,' Mr LeBoeff said. 'As you can see, Hélène and I had done some work to put our plan into action. A friend of a friend was closing down an atelier in London. We bought everything and had it shipped here. Carrying it down the stairs was extra,' he said with a wry smile.

'It's – amazing.'

'We bought it with the school in mind. But it should work perfectly well for you to expand the shop.' He pointed to the clothing racks and mannequins. 'And if you can put them to use, then please do so.'

I'd stared at him in disbelief. 'But you could sell them. Get money for them. Shop fittings are expensive. I . . . I couldn't pay you.'

He shook his head. 'For me, Andrea, it is not about the money. Use them to help your mother. Make your dream happen. And God bless you.' The tears were back in his eyes. 'It is what Hélène would have wanted. I couldn't do it. But you can.'

It seemed like some kind of bizarre dream where I'd woken up and become Cinderella, with a fairy godfather – a Frenchman who owns a chippie. I climbed the stairs and started babbling again about my ideas.

'We can make it just like a real . . . what do you call it – a-tell-i-er?' I said.

'*Atelier*,' he corrected me.

'Clients can come into the studios and see their clothing being made. And in the main shop, each designer will have their little space – like in the *Great British Bake Off* tent. There will also be a place for the vintage consignment stuff – that's Mum's territory.'

'Yes,' he enthused. 'You must not overlook the wonderful innovation of the past. The great designers that are the foundation of everything that came after – what we call modern.'

'Yeah . . .' I said. 'Like Hélène's things—'

I broke off, worried that I'd put my foot in it again. Because in all my blathering, there was one little thing I'd held back. One little *important* thing. The fact that I had sold the polka-dot dress that belonged to Hélène, and that Thomas was giving me some of her handbags and shoes to sell to get money for the paint and renovations.

I looked over at Mr LeBoeff. His smile didn't falter, and for a second I thought I'd got away with it.

'Ah yes, Hélène's things.' He sighed deeply. 'Some of them are very valuable – one-of-a-kind pieces.'

'Yeah,' I squawked.

'It is another thing that I have not been able to face in all these years. It was a comfort, I suppose, to hold on to them.'

'I understand.'

He shook his head sadly. 'It is a waste to have it as it is now. She would not have wanted it that way. Her things should be seen, worn – loved, as they once were.'

'Well, the shop would be perfect for that,' I say in a small voice. 'I mean, you'd get the money and everything.' I think about the conversation I had with Thomas about the 'split'. If I were to sell Hélène's things at the shop, I'd do it for nothing. I'd do it as a labour of love.

He laughed. 'You will need money to go ahead with your plans. You may have a vision, but without more it will never come to anything. I will keep a few of her things. Things that are special to me. But you must sell the rest and take a percentage. Do you think you can do that?'

'Um, I think so.' I forced a note of doubt into my voice. 'If you're sure . . .'

'I think the time has come,' he said. 'So, yes . . .' He swallowed hard. 'I am sure.'

'That's great – I mean, thank you so much,' I said, feeling overcome by his generosity. But he didn't seem to hear me. He stared across the expanse of the theatre but his eyes were far away. Was he picturing his wife here, as they'd planned all along? A last glimpse of the woman he had married, in her beautiful clothes, before things went all wrong?

Or was he thinking about the future and what we could create here?

'Um, there is one thing . . .' I said quietly, not sure if I was disturbing him. 'Mum will want to know about the business arrangements. I mean, you own all this and she has just a little corner.'

He shook his head, still half in his own world. 'Of course, when she returns, I will speak to Eliza.' For a second, a light went into his eyes and I wondered . . . but no. There couldn't be anything between him and Mum. I mean . . . could there? They're both about the same age, and as he'd said before, they're shop neighbours. I wonder if Thomas has noticed anything . . .

'But in the meantime,' he continued, 'this project belongs to you and Thomas. I will trust you both to do what is fair.'

We'd left it at that − shaking hands, and me promising to give him a copy of the business plan I'd written for school, and let him know if I needed anything. He'd gone out through the velvet curtain, still muttering to himself. I stayed in the theatre for a while longer, standing in the centre of the room, visualizing exactly what I wanted to do. Then I walked through the archway to Mum's shop to see if Stevie and Carrie were still there. They weren't — they must have left when I was down looking at the mannequins. I checked my watch — I really needed to go as well so I wouldn't be late to dinner at Stevie's. As I was walking back across the theatre, I heard a noise in the corridor at the back.

Footsteps.

My heart beats faster. Even though I've made things right with Mr LeBoeff — something we should have done weeks ago — I just know that Thomas is going to be mad. I've betrayed his 'secret' to his uncle. It seemed to go well, but he may not see it that way.

The curtain parts. The person who comes through is tall with streaked orange and blonde hair. Not Thomas.

Jolanta.

The one person I wasn't expecting, and yet, the one person who might be able to provide the final missing piece.

30

ONE FOOT IN FRONT OF THE OTHER

'Hi, Jolanta, how's it going?' I give her a friendly smile.

She looks surprised to see me – and not in a good way. 'I was looking for your mum,' she says. 'To make sure she is OK. But no one's at the shop. I saw the door open here. I thought Thomas might be—' Her eyes move around the room and settle on the knocked-down wall. 'Oh, Andy, what have you done?'

'It's a long story.' I mean to continue with an apology, but the next thing out of my mouth is: 'How do you know Thomas?'

She laughs – obviously she can tell that I'm jealous. I hold my breath, expecting her to tease me. But to her credit, she doesn't.

'He came to the shop a while back,' she says. 'He asked me to come over and take a look at his aunt's things. He wanted to know if they were valuable.' She shakes her head. 'I had never seen anything like them before. So . . . amazing.'

'Yeah,' I say. 'They are.'

She gives me a sideways glance, and for a second I'm sure she's on to me and the fact that I took the white bag. If she saw the bag, she might well have recognized the things for what they were.

'But what are *you* doing here, Andy?' she says. 'And what happened to the wall?'

I decide then and there that I'm going to tell her. My problem with Jolanta before was that I felt jealous of how close she was to Mum. But having her on-side could be a major bonus.

'I'm fixing up *Eliza's Emporium*,' I say. 'I'm going to turn it into something really special.'

'You?' she frowns. 'Where's Eliza?'

'Mum's, um . . . away,' I say. 'Having a break. She needed to get some perspective on things. The shop was failing before — that's why she let you go.'

'I know.'

'Anyway, what I'm doing is a surprise. I'm giving the shop a makeover. Thomas is helping me, and some other friends are helping too. Mr LeBoeff – he knows about it. And actually . . .' I take a breath. 'I have a business proposition for you too.'

'Oh?'

'Yeah.' I stammer on with telling her my plan. 'I was wondering if you – and some of the other students at the fashion college – might need studio space. And a place to sell your designs.' I outline my idea. Her expression goes from one of thought, to disbelief, to interest.

'And you think this could work – this idea you have?' Doubt seems to be the force that wins out.

'I don't see why not. We'd be selling vintage, but also new designs. The best of old and new.'

She laughs then, but not in a mean way. 'How old are you, Andy?' she says.

'Thirteen,' I say proudly.

To my surprise, Jolanta nods. 'That is how old I was when I came to this country,' she says. 'I know that thirteen is old enough to do many things. Transform a shop?' She shrugs. 'Why not?'

'I'd really like to have you on board, Jolanta,' I say. 'I know you liked working here – liked working for Mum.'

'Your mum is a very good person. She is also talented, and knows very much. It made me angry before – that you didn't seem to appreciate that.'

'Maybe not.' I realize that she's right. I've never consciously thought of Mum as 'talented'. Just another thing I overlooked because it was right under my nose. 'And you're right, I should have done. But hopefully, it's not too late.'

Jolanta doesn't answer but she nods her head. To me, that's enough.

As I walk back to Stevie's house, my mind feels like a cauldron about to bubble over. I'm glad Jolanta didn't say my idea was rubbish – and it would be good to have her help. But the worries are there too, waiting in the shadows. What about Mum? What about Thomas? What is fair? Am I going to fail? Will Thomas ever forgive me? Will Mum?

When I reach Stevie's house, I hear laughter coming from inside. Someone – Carrie? – says: 'Come on, one more go – you can do it!' Clapping in rhythm. An almighty groaning sound.

I'm almost afraid to go inside, but I *live* here for now, so I don't have much choice. I get the key from under the mat and let myself in. I open the door. In the front room, the coffee table and sofa have been pushed to one side and there's a contraption there like the parallel bars that men do flips on in the Olympics. Stevie's wheelchair is positioned between the bars. Carrie is bent down on the floor by Stevie's feet, and behind her, helping to keep her lifted out of the chair – is Thomas. I watch as Carrie helps her move her left foot forward. Stevie's skinny arms wobble as she tries to keep herself upright. Thomas grips her by the waist. It's painful to watch as Stevie moves her left foot a few centimetres, and drags her other foot forward. Thomas lets go for a second. 'You can do it!' Carrie says.

'Arrugh!' Stevie cries out.

'You're doing great!' I yell.

Thomas turns round and sees me. Stevie yelps and falls back on her bottom into the chair.

'Hi,' I say, as everyone glares at me. 'Sorry for interrupting.'

'Andy!' Stevie says. 'I'm doing it. I've taken three steps! All by myself.' She glances at Thomas and her face turns tomato red. 'Well, sort of.'

'That's fantastic,' I say. 'Can I help?'

'Get down and guide her right foot,' Thomas says.

'But I'm knackered,' Stevie says.

'You wanted to take five steps,' Thomas says firmly. 'So that's two more, Einstein. Now let's get cracking.'

'One foot in front of the other,' Carrie cheers. 'That's all you have to do!'

'That's all?!' Stevie gasps as she tries to lift herself out of the chair. I crouch down as Thomas helps steady her as best he can. Her left leg is shaking as she tries to put weight on it. I grip her right ankle. 'One, two, three . . .' I give a tug and she judders forward.

'OK, now left,' Thomas directs.

Stevie takes another step and this time, remains standing for almost a whole second by herself before teetering backwards. The three of us help her into her chair.

'I'm so proud of you,' I say, giving her a hug. I turn to Thomas. 'Thank you.'

For a second he stares at me, his smile brief. 'My pleasure, Andy.' His eyes are almost black as they hold mine. In that one tiny moment, the whole world seems to shimmer and spin except for him – solid and real – right in front of me.

'Now,' Carrie says, 'who'd like something to eat?'

The moment passes. I go to the kitchen and help Carrie finish making dinner – a big pot of spaghetti, tomato sauce and salad. When the food is ready, we all sit down around the table to brainstorm ideas for the shop.

'I think we need a new name,' I say. '*Eliza's Emporium* is just so . . . tired.'

'But what about your mum?' Carrie says. 'Won't she be upset if you change it?'

'Maybe.' Her pointing it out gives me a little flash of guilt.

'You've knocked out a whole wall and got rid of half of her precious stock,' Stevie says. 'I think the name is the least of her worries.'

'I agree,' Thomas says. 'New start – new name. You'll also need a really hip logo.'

'How about UpStreet!?' Stevie suggests. 'It combines two of your essential components – high street and upmarket. You could use an upwards arrow for the logo.'

'Hmmm.' I narrow my eyes. 'When I figure out what "essential components" means, I'll let you know.'

'It's a start.' Thomas says. 'But the "street" part might put off your older clientele. You need something classy.'

'We need the ladies who buy the baggy sweaters,' I say. 'At least for now. So it will need to appeal to them too.'

'What about the design bit?' Carrie says. 'I thought that was your USP.'

'USP?' I look around for something I can pelt

her with.

'It stands for "unique selling point".' Carrie smiles proudly. 'There was a show on – some lady who transforms dodgy old high streets into places people want to go.'

'Hey, Einstein II,' Thomas says playfully, 'that's good. A unique selling point.'

Carrie blushes at the compliment.

'Well, it sounds like gibberish to me,' I say, 'but before we figure it out, I'd better tell you another idea I had.' I go on to explain my new plan – getting fashion students and young designers to sell their stuff in part of the shop, and having Mum sell nice vintage stuff and consignment stuff in the other part.'

'That's interesting,' Thomas says, looking slightly puzzled. 'When did you come up with that?'

'Um . . . just now. I mean, earlier today. I came to find you, but you weren't at the chippie. Instead, I . . .'

He's staring at me now, and I can feel the familiar itch of guilt at the fact that I'm always keeping things back. I take a breath. He's going to find out soon enough, so I may as well tell him.

'. . . I talked to your uncle,' I say.

One by one, mouths that were about to speak

close up. 'Oh,' Stevie squeaks. She puts a hand over her lips.

Thomas stands up like he owes it to himself to storm out. Then he sits back down, arms folded. 'And?' he says.

'And we had a nice chat,' I say. 'As you told me, your Aunt Hélène wanted to use the theatre as a school – a place to teach young up-and-coming designers. Mr LeBoeff agreed a school wasn't very practical. But we can still bring Hélène's vision to life. We can create something amazing.'

Thomas glares at me but says nothing. Luckily my friends bridge the silence.

'So the USP is designer fashion,' Stevie says.

'Classic and modern,' Carrie adds.

I wait. For Thomas to digest what I've said. For him to decide he's mad at me – or not. If he's still in – or not. Mr LeBoeff was very clear that what happens next is between Thomas and me to sort out. I definitely haven't handled everything right, and he's so strong-willed that I know he won't let me get away with anything. I watch the emotions move across his face like dark clouds on the horizon.

'What do you think, Thomas?' Stevie takes the plunge.

Thomas looks at her and seems to soften. 'I

have no idea what to think,' he says, shaking his head. 'No idea whether it will work or not.' He turns back to me. 'But I can see, Andy, that no matter what I say, you're going to give it a go.'

But I'm barely listening to him. An image has popped into my head. An image of me – the older, more sophisticated me – twirling in front of the mirror in the polka-dot dress. Classy and timeless, modern and fun.

'*The Polka Dot Shop*,' I say.

'What?' Carrie says.

'*The Polka Dot Shop*. We'll have a logo in black with big white polka dots like the Chanel dress. It's such a classic design, but it's fun too – it will be perfect. What do you think?' I look around to each of my friends in turn. Everyone nods their heads.

'I love it,' Stevie says.

'Me too!' Carrie echoes.

Thomas gives me a long, unreadable look. 'It just might work.'

31

THE POLKA DOT SHOP

Time flies by – I can't remember ever being so busy. At lunchtime over the next few days, Stevie, Carrie and I make endless to-do lists. After school, it's up to me to get on with things. A few days after meeting Jolanta at the theatre, I get on a bus and go to visit her at the fashion college. It takes me over an hour to get there because the bus makes about a thousand stops. By the time I get there I'm frustrated and second-guessing everything again. But when she meets me at the door and takes me inside, all of a sudden I feel a new jolt of energy.

The corridor looks like a normal school, but the classrooms are totally different. There's a huge space – almost as big as the theatre – which is flooded with light from windows on one side. It's filled with mannequins, work tables, sewing machines, computer tablets, mood boards, and pinned-up sketches. A whole wall is covered with rolls of beautiful fabrics in all different colours and textures, and there are trays full of buttons, and rolls of trims and ribbons.

Three students – two women and a man – are working on projects. The man is making some kind of elaborate dress out of cut-up beer cans and wool on a dress form, one woman is cutting out luxurious silk fabric from a hand-drawn pattern, and the other woman is hemming a drapey satin dress on a mannequin. It looks like something a Greek goddess might wear. I experience a strange pull of longing in my chest. I wish I knew how to sew and design clothes. I've always been pretty good at drawing – and most importantly, I know what kind of clothes I like. Maybe it's something I could think about for the future.

The next hour is a blur. Jolanta introduces me to some of her student friends and I tell them about my idea – studio space at the back of the theatre for a small rent, and the right to sell their designs in the shop. We'd take a commission (I haven't worked out actual numbers yet, but

Thomas says I should get at least forty per cent) on any sales. 'We're going to call it *The Polka Dot Shop*,' I tell them. 'The name was inspired by a beautiful Chanel dress. It's going to be classic, and modern, and retro and fun. That's our vision.'

Surprisingly, no one seems too bothered that I'm only thirteen, and five people show a definite interest. I take their names and email addresses, and agree to get in touch with final details.

Before I leave, Jolanta introduces me to one of her professors – a woman who once ran a consignment shop in London. She tells me some of the tricks of the trade as far as getting good stock, and also tells me a few home truths. I'm not expecting it to be easy, but she definitely gives me a lot of things to think about.

'You need the shop to become a *destination*,' she says. 'And that won't be easy. You'll need money, and publicity – and most importantly, the best stock. You'll need to give people a reason to come, a reason to browse, and a reason to buy.'

'That's exactly what I want to do.' I tell her my ideas about eventually opening a café and fashion bookshop alongside the fashion shop. 'It will be a place for people who love fashion,' I say. 'That's our USP.' I've practised saying the letters until they roll off my tongue. 'Whether you're into vintage, or cutting-edge new designs, you can find it at *The Polka Dot Shop*.'

'I love the name,' she says. But then, the next thing I know, she's asking me The Question.

'How old are you, Andy?'

'Thirteen.'

'I'll give you this – you've definitely got guts.' She smiles at me. 'And in this business, that's a good thing. You might just succeed.'

With this vote of confidence from someone knowledgeable, I feel like I'm floating on air.

When I'm finished talking to the professor, Jolanta walks with me to the bus stop. 'I'm really sorry, Jolanta,' I say. 'About how I treated you before. I guess I was just jealous because you were so close to Mum.' I purse my lips. 'And by the way, I did take that white bag.' Her blue eyes narrow as I tell her about how I found the bag, and sold the polka-dot dress on eBay. I tell her that I used the money on paint for the shop, and the rest of the stuff in the bag I gave back to Thomas.'

'I knew it,' she says when I've finished. 'It was awkward for me telling your mum, but when I found that bag on the doorstep I was very excited. I really thought those things might have been able to save the shop.' She cocks her head. 'But I suppose it *was* too good to be true. I thought I recognized some of the things Thomas showed me.'

'Do you think Mum could have sold them for anything like what they're worth?'

'No.' She shakes her head. 'I really like your mum, but she's not very good at business, is she?'

'No.' I smile. 'That's where I come in.'

By the time I get back on the bus, I'm tired, and my brain is ready to burst. It feels good to have made up with Jolanta, and to have found a few more allies. As the bus rumbles on, I can feel something bubbling up inside my chest. Excitement about what I'm doing. And something else too – confidence. More than I've ever felt before.

32

A BLANK CANVAS

My new-found confidence waxes and wanes over the next week as I try to get on with the checklist. Stevie helps me crunch the numbers on the consignment operation, and the professor at Jolanta's fashion college confirms that a forty–sixty split, while generous (we're the ones who get the forty per cent) should attract better stock. She agrees to help put out the word, and Jolanta's boyfriend – who happens to be some kind of IT whizz – helps out too. He shows us how to add a cool background in black-and-white polka dots to our eBay shop. (We've set up a new account now for The Polka Dot Shop, that Jolanta is looking after since she's over eighteen.)

He also helps us set up social media accounts on Facebook and Twitter and a shop portal on Etsy. He also works with us on a design for our business cards and the bags for the shop – I want to have nice paper bags with cord handles like at the *Galeries Lafayette*, with our polka-dot logo on the sides.

I put Stevie in charge of social media, stock sorting and pricing, while Carrie and I get on with clearing out Mum's shop. Thomas helps us with the biggest and dirtiest job – getting rid of the nasty old carpet and sanding down the wood floor with a huge round sander from a tool rental place. It takes hours – the sandpaper band keeps breaking – and by the time we're done, there's fine wooden sawdust in every pore of my body. Then it takes another whole evening to varnish the floor to a high gloss. Doing the floor makes all of us – even Stevie – dirty, tired and irritable. But when I go into the shop the next day, I'm amazed by how beautiful the wooden parquet is – just like in the theatre. The varnish is smooth and glossy, practically like a mirror. We cover the whole floor with a cloth, and then get on with painting the walls. It's a lot easier than the theatre, and we get both coats done in a single evening. We also paint the front door – I get a particular glow of satisfaction when I smear over the 'New to U' logo with a wide swathe of black paint!

The next night, Thomas helps us refit the racks and rails for hanging the clothes. He also builds some fitting room cubicles out of plywood that we found in the basement of the old theatre, and the four of us hang giant full-length mirrors inside. Thomas lets us have some of the old black velvet curtains from the theatre, and Jolanta and Carrie cut them down so that they fit over the dressing room doors, tied back with fancy-looking ropes of pearls that we salvage from Mum's stock.

Most satisfying of all is filling the skip behind the chippie with all of the old, worn-out things – carpet, rubble, and the worst of the old clothes from *Eliza's Emporium*. In going through the clothing on the over-crowded racks, we've actually found quite a few hidden gems. There are tops and skirts from high-street shops, suits from department stores and some elegant little black dresses.

I have to confess that some of the things we find, I actually want to try on and wear. I offer Stevie and Carrie the chance to pick out one or two things as 'payment' for their help. Stevie takes a skirt and a pair of trousers ('these will look good for walking') and Carrie finds a nice T-shirt from Ted Baker and a pair of pink Converse. (Who knew that all along she was liking my 'pre-loved' Converse?) I take a few things too – a denim (yes, denim!) skirt, and a couple of tops. It's not exactly a shopping spree at Westfield, but it's OK.

We arrange everything we're keeping for the shop by size and colour. I also keep an eye out for anything that might suit Ms Cartwright – like I said I would. The rest of the stuff – anything that looks stained, worn or too tatty – we put in bin bags. (We make a separate rack of 'fancy dress' clothing that we can hire out if people want it. I put the seventies velvet suit on the rack, along with the gold prom dress. The Hawaiian outfit, though, went to the skip.)

In the end, I chicken out and don't toss the bin bags of cast-offs – just in case Mum gets sentimental over the old stuff. Instead, we take them to the very back of the theatre basement. If Mum wants something, she'll have to go and find it!

At the end of the second week, when we've finished painting, Stevie bars me from the shop for Sunday evening – Thomas is working at the chippie, Carrie isn't home yet from boot camp, and Stevie wants to talk numbers. Not hardcore quantum physics or calculus or whatever it is she does – but about the shop.

We sit in her bedroom and go through the facts and figures that Stevie has come up with for the business plan, and the names of people who have responded to my advert in the local paper and on our new Facebook page for designer clothing wanted on consignment. I also check my eBay auctions – which I've set up to raise money for the paint and the floor sander, not to mention the endless pizza and Diet Cokes we seem to be going through. I've listed more of Thomas's aunt's clothing, shoes and handbags, which Jolanta's helped me sort through. We're selling the things that are nice but not one-of-a-kind – those we're keeping to use for publicity at the grand opening. Before I list anything, I'm making sure to check with Thomas or his uncle. (Mr LeBoeff has cried over one or two things we've found, and I felt really sad for him. But I think what we're doing truly is helping him come to terms with the fact that Hélène is gone.)

All in all, I've managed to make over £1200 – which to me seems like a fortune – but we're nearly through it already. Everything seems to cost so much. Stevie's making sure I keep records of every penny we spend and every penny we make – to keep the taxman happy, she says. I don't know anything about that, but I try to do what she says.

I'm just about to shut down the computer and get ready for bed when the phone in Stevie's room rings. 'Can you get it?' she says, waving in my direction.

'Sure.'

I answer it, my heart doing a little flip when I hear Thomas's voice. 'Andy, is that you?'

'Yeah. You OK?'

'Can you and Einstein come over to the shop?'

'What, now?'

'Yeah, now.' An unusual hesitation in his voice makes me a little scared. 'It's . . . important,' he says. Then he hangs up.

I tell Stevie what he said. 'We'd better sneak out the front,' she says. 'I don't think my parents will like us going out so late.'

'OK.'

We put on our coats and leave the house. The night is silent except for the sound of distant traffic and an owl hooting from the rafters. Clouds wisp slowly across the moon. I don't know what's up – and I always seem to fear the worst – but somehow, what I feel most is a sense of anticipation. Knowing that I'm about to see Thomas has that effect on me, I guess.

The high street is deserted by the time we

reach it. At one point, Stevie stops and drafts a quick text on her phone. At the end of the parade of shops, *Eliza's Emporium* is dark.

As we pass the old theatre, Stevie stops again.

'What are you—' I say. 'Oh!—'

I gasp as all of a sudden a light blinds my eyes. The inside of Mum's shop lights up — a pure white space with chrome fittings and sparkling windows. Running along the top of each wall is a black strip of paint about ten centimetres deep, with fresh white-painted polka dots. Above the door, there's a black sign, also with white polka dots. Clear white light-up lettering says: *The Polka Dot Shop*. Everything looks new and fresh, and expensive — a blank canvas for a whole new venture. The shop looks classic and modern, time-less and fun — all at the same time. A shop that's going to succeed.

'It's wonderful!' I cry.

The door opens from inside. Thomas is there, along with Carrie, Jolanta and her boyfriend. 'Surprise!' they say in unison.

I rush up to Thomas and throw my arms around his neck. Everyone's had a hand in what's been done, but without him — and that night when I found him in the back of Mum's shop looking for the white bag — none of it ever would have happened. And there have been so many ups and down, twists and turns between us — at any point he could have shattered my dreams with an angry, unforgiving word. But he didn't, and instead, I have . . . this. Someone whistles and I come to my senses. Blushing and flustered, I give Carrie, Stevie and Jolanta hugs in turn.

'It looks amazing,' I say.

They've hung the leftover velvet curtain at the sides of the archway that leads to the old theatre. The theatre itself is dark, but the freshly painted white walls seem to glow from within. Mum's shop has been fully fitted out like a high-end clothing boutique. The dressing rooms look chic, as do the chrome railings and shelves — even the old counter with the till has been painted a glossy black. In the centre is a white rectangle with black polka dots and lettering that says *The Polka Dot Shop*. I'd seen much of the work in progress, of course, but seeing the place cleaned up, cleared out, sparkling and ready for business is a huge surprise, as are the polka dots!

Ready, that is, except for the fact that there's nothing in the shop to sell.

'Come and see the back,' Stevie says. She takes my hand and propels her chair forward, pulling me along.

We go through the curtain at the back that leads to the old stockroom. It too has been cleaned and painted, and the shelves cleared. The little kitchen area is tidy, and there are new white mugs hanging on a rack above the sink. A brand-new kettle is on the countertop. Mum's sewing area has been moved neatly to one corner, along with two sewing mannequins, a desk lamp, and an ironing board that folds down from the wall.

'I can't believe it's the same place,' I say, grinning. 'Anyone fancy a cup of something?'

Thomas has already thought of that and stocked the little fridge with Diet Cokes and water. He tosses us each a drink and together we gather in the centre of the floor and raise our bottles and cans for a toast.

'To bin bags,' Thomas says, winking at me.

'To amazing friends,' I say.

'To polka dots,' Stevie chimes in.

'To success!' Carrie says.

'Here, here!' we clink our bottles and cans.

'Thank you so much.' My eyes overflow with joyful tears.

33

THE PRODIGAL MUM

The next morning when I wake up in Stevie's spare room, I remember the night before and half expect that I'm still dreaming. I can't believe how the shop has been transformed – it's like *Eliza's Emporium* never existed. But, as the phone rings next to the bed and a familiar number comes up on the display, I realize with a flash of guilt that it did – and still does – exist to one very important person: Mum.

'Andy?' Mum sounds breathless as I pick up the phone. 'I wanted to catch you before you left for school.'

'Hi, Mum,' I say. 'You all right?'

I wait for the hesitation that seems to come

each time I ask this. But this time, she replies instantly. 'Yes, Andy, I'm fabulous.'

'Really? That's good, Mum.'

'Yes, and what's more, I have news.'

'What is it?' I ignore a tiny flicker of alarm.

'I think you'll be pleased, Andy. I've had such a lovely time up here – seeing everyone, being with family, going for long walks. I've done a lot of thinking.'

Thinking = bad. I just know it.

'What about?'

'About our future, of course! I've found this lovely old barn – just a hop, skip and a jump from the high street.'

'A barn?' My stomach clenches.

'I could expand the *Emporium*. There would be so much more space. I'm coming to realize how cramped everything is. I could add loads more stock – get everything out of the bags in the back. I could have a little studio to do alterations – you know, like the buttons I put on that cardigan you sold.' She breathes in swiftly. 'I mean, the barn would need a little work, but I could get a bank loan – or something. The main thing is – it would be a whole new start.'

'But Mum . . . it's . . . in the Lake District.' My whole life flashes before my eyes. I mean, we may have had problems, but we had stability – if that's the right word.

Through the phone line I feel the energy go flat. 'But . . .' Mum sputters, 'you were the one who told me to come up here.'

'Yes, for a holiday! That's hardly the same thing. I mean – I have school, and friends, and . . .' I don't dare say his name, but it's his face, his blue-grey eyes that flash into my mind like a firework.

There's silence on the end of the line. For a long second, I worry I've gone way too far. Mum was trying to make things better – move forward. Have I messed that up?

'I mean, there are some good things about the idea,' I stammer quickly. 'More space would be good. Things wouldn't be squished on the racks. And the bank loan. A little money might go a long way. It's just – I don't know. A barn? The Lake District? Do they "*do*" the whole vintage thing up there?'

She exhales sharply. 'I thought you'd be happy.'

'I am! I mean – I want you to be happy.'

'Do you, Andy – do you really?'

'Well . . . of course I do. We just need to think about the options, that's all.'

'The options?' To my relief, she laughs. 'You sound like a grown-up – not a thirteen-year-old.'

I bristle. It always comes down to the fact that I'm thirteen, therefore she – an adult – must know best. It's not only irritating, but in this case, just plain wrong.

'You could come up here – see the place for yourself.'

'Um . . .' I picture a 'new and improved' *Eliza's Emporium* in some old barn up in the Lake District. Acres of space – for people's old welly boots caked with mud; moth-eaten old tartan coats that have been stored in the loft for decades; stacks of used jeans; second-hand thermal under-wear . . .'The problem is, Mum, I'm really busy at school right now. Maybe you should come back for a while, and then we could go up together in the summer.'

'School.' Her bracelets jangle dismissively in the background. 'Yes, I suppose you're right. You've got school. I've up and left you . . .'

'Really, Mum, it's been fine. I'm just looking forward to having you back. I've missed you lots.'

As soon as I say it, I realize how much I do miss her. She's my mum, and until now, we haven't been separated. Yes, I've been busy, but I miss her hugs, hearing her talk about her day, and knowing that she's there when I go to bed at night.

'I've missed you too, Andy. More than you

know. And you're right. It's time I came home. I'll get a train back. Probably the day after tomorrow. There's a late train that evening.' She sighs. 'Time to get back to the real world.'

'OK, Mum,' I say. 'Can't wait to see you. Love you.'

'Love you too.'

'And, Mum . . .' There's a click.

'I have a surprise for you too,' I say into the dead line.

34

AN EMERGENCY MEETING

That night, I call an emergency meeting of 'Team Polka Dot Shop'. We meet in the old theatre. The wall lights have all been repaired and they cast a gentle glow over the vast white space.

'Mum's coming home the day after tomorrow,' I say. 'And what's more, she's thinking of moving to the Lake District.'

'What, just like that?' Stevie says.

'She can't,' Carrie says. 'I mean – you've got to have a say in it too, right?'

'I'm thirteen years old,' I intone in Mum's voice. 'I don't have a say in anything.'

Dangling his legs over the stage, Thomas is the

only one who doesn't look upset. In his paint-splattered T-shirt and jeans, his hair curling just above his shoulders, he looks gorgeous.

'This is a good thing,' he says.

'What?' The three of us look at him.

'Your mum is up for a change – that's what you want. She may not know what the change is – so now you'll point her in the right direction. Or in this case, you've done a little more than just point.'

A thousand reasons he's wrong pop into my head, but my friends have done so much work, I don't want to disappoint them. 'I'm just worried that I'm not ready,' I say. 'I mean – the shop looks lovely – amazing. But we've got nothing in it.'

He smiles at me then, full of confidence and self-assurance. 'So, you'd better get ready.'

He swings off the stage and gestures for Carrie and I to follow him. Just before he reaches the curtain he turns around and tosses Stevie his mobile phone. 'Call your mum, Einstein. Tell her you won't be home for dinner.'

Thomas doesn't bother to explain his latest scheme. Instead, he herds Carrie to the back of the theatre and the door that leads to the space under the stage. 'We'll bring up some extra fittings and mannequins,' he says.

I stop, hands on my hips. 'What am I going to do?' I ask.

He holds out his set of keys. 'Well, unless you've got some more hidden gems squirrelled away in the back of your mum's shop, I'd say, get some of Hélène's things out.'

'Really?' Carrie says.

I take the keys. 'Are you sure about this, Thomas?'

He looks up at me and smiles. 'Yes, Andy, I'm sure. Find some things you think your mum could sell in the shop. We can hang them on the racks so she can see what the place is going to look like.'

'So you mean we'll do it like a stage set?'

He nods. 'Show her how it could look if we went with your idea of different sections for vintage, new designs and vintage-inspired designs.'

'OK,' I say, smiling back. 'I'll have a go.'

We spend the rest of the evening working on restocking. We put out the hidden gems we've found from Mum's stock, and also go through some of Hélène's things and hang them on the racks. As lovely as Hélène's things are, though, I can't help but feel that something's missing. The centrepiece for the window display that I'm picturing in my mind. And it's my fault that it's missing. I don't tell the others though. Not until I've tried to make it right.

When we finally call it a night and get back to Stevie's house, I'm practically asleep on my feet with exhaustion. Stevie is not only tired, but also in pain from the walking practice. I help her into bed, but before I turn out the light, I ask if I can use her iPad.

'Sure,' she says. 'What's up?'

'I just want to check our eBay auctions,' I say. (Checking the bids on the things we're selling has become one of my new favourite hobbies.)

'OK – sure,' she says. 'Goodnight.'

I unplug the iPad from its charger and take it to the sofa bed. I log into eBay and the original seller account that I created. I click on the messages section and type in a new message: to the buyer of the polka-dot dress.

35

THE UNVEILING

When I wake up three days later on Stevie's sofa bed, I'm twisted inside out with nerves. Today's the day when all will be revealed to the one person who matters most – Mum.

No one else is awake yet, so I dress quickly, write a thank-you note to Stevie and her mum and dad, then heft my rucksack on to my back. It takes me ten minutes to walk home, and every step of the way I worry. Mum's train was due to arrive late last night. If, for some reason, she's already up and about, the surprise might be ruined.

When I reach our house, I fish out my key and

open the door. For a second, it feels strange to be back in my own home. But as soon as I see Mum's shoes — pink-and-white striped espadrilles — by the door and hear the shower running upstairs, I feel a lot better. Mum's home!

I go into the kitchen and see that Mum's bought a bag of groceries. I put on a pot of coffee for her and force myself to eat a piece of toast. I hear the sound of the water go off and her moving about in her room. I tidy up the kitchen and pour cereal into a bowl for her.

Eventually she comes down. 'Andy!' she says, holding out her arms.

I run into them. We squeeze each other tightly, and tears form in my eyes as I breathe in the familiar scent of sandalwood and rose.

'I'm so happy to see you,' I say.

'It's good to be back.' She holds me at arm's length and looks me over. 'Have you grown taller?' she says, ruffling my hair.

'In three weeks?'

'You look like a model,' she says.

'Hardly.' I laugh, gesturing down to my jeans and black T-shirt. The jeans were another 'find' from when we were clearing out the shop. They were brand-new — still had a tag on them. The top is one I took as 'payment'. It wasn't new, but even the fashion police can't give the thumbs down to a plain black T-shirt.

'No, really.' Mum's face is serious. 'I think we need to start aiming higher, Andy. We're just as good as other people. We need to start believing it.'

'I totally agree,' I say. Mum may have been reading a few too many self-help books while she's been away, but I hope that she means it. What had Thomas said? *So now you'll point her in the right direction.*

'In fact, Andy, I've been doing some thinking about what you said before I left. About getting in some really good stock, and raising the prices. I like putting bespoke touches on some of the pieces, and those ought to cost a little more. Whether we stay here, or move up north, I think those ideas have some merit.'

'Really?' I feel like a light has gone on inside me. The fact that she's taking my ideas seriously means so much. Smiling, I take her hand and lead her over to the table. 'Sit down,' I say. 'I made you a welcome home breakfast.' I bring her the cereal bowl and a cup of fresh coffee. 'I'm so glad that you're back.'

'Me too, sweetheart.' Her smile looks genuine – almost like her old self. 'Now, I want to hear about everything you've been up to.'

'Well, I *have* been busy . . .'

I hover as Mum finishes her breakfast. I've managed to convince her that all I've been doing in the last few weeks is hanging out with my friends, helping Stevie with her walking, and going for after-school jogs with Carrie. But now that it's almost time to tell her the truth, I feel dizzy with nerves.

Mum checks her watch and gives me a concerned look. 'Don't you have school, Andy?'

'Um, it's an inset morning,' I lie. 'I thought I'd come with you to the shop. There's something I want to show you.'

'The shop?' Concern turns to wariness. 'I assume the shop is just the way I left it. I took the key so no one could break in.'

'Did you?' I don't meet her eyes. 'OK – just let me know when you're ready to go.'

As we walk to the shop, Mum chats about the Lake District. It's a little off-putting, but I nod my head and say: 'I'm glad you had a good rest, Mum.' I cut in and start talking about school before she can mention the 'quaint old barn' she found. As we turn on to the high street, I tell her about the special project that Ms Cartwright gave us.

We pass the betting shop.

'We're supposed to make something better in our lives,' I say. 'We're supposed to be a little braver. Take a risk . . .'

We pass the funeral parlour.

'That sounds like a worthy goal,' Mum says. 'What did you choose?'

We pass the chippie.

'Well . . . you'll see.'

Mum stops dead in her tracks. She lets out a little scream. Her hands grip my arm, fingers digging into my skin. 'Oh, Andy,' she says. 'What's happened? Where's *Eliza's Emporium*?' She squints against the sun. '*The Polka Dot Shop*? What on earth is that?'

Mr LeBoeff comes out of the chippie. Thomas is just behind him, looking a little bit like a deer in the headlights.

'Eliza!' Mr LeBoeff says. 'Welcome home!' He kisses her on both cheeks. 'You must see what wonderful things these young people have been up to!'

'I . . . I . . .' Mum clutches her chest, her face bright pink.

I lead her forwards. 'Come and see, Mum. Before you say anything, just come and see.'

Mr LeBoeff and Thomas follow from a distance as I lead her up to the window. She puts her hand over her mouth in shock. 'What is this? I mean, it's a designer shop or something. It's not . . . mine.'

Worry stabs my chest. Does she not like it? It looks so stylish and beautiful and we worked so hard. How can she *not* like it?

'It *is* yours,' I say. 'Here, give me your key. I'll show you.'

She fumbles in her pocket and draws the key out with a trembling hand. The panes of glass in the newly painted door sparkle like gems in the morning light. The key fits and turns in the lock. Mum's jaw gapes open, and it's almost like she's afraid to go inside.

'Let me switch on the lights.'

I go in before her and flip the switch by the till. The white space floods with light. The chrome dazzles, and the clothing on the racks – not very much, if I'm honest – looks neat and expensive. The polka-dot border and logo are classy and fun.

As soon as Mum's inside, she seems to revive. Like a kid in a sweet shop she rushes from one rack to the other, flipping through the clothing. 'Where on earth did these things come from?' she says half to herself.

'Um, from Mr LeBoeff.'

Mum turns back, as if noticing for the first time that we're not alone.

'It's all vintage designer clothing that belonged to his wife,' I say. 'She was called *La Belle Hélène*.'

'And now I am glad that it has finally found a use,' Mr LeBoeff says. He wipes a tear from his eye. 'It is exactly what she would have wanted.'

Mum goes up to him and grabs his hand. 'I don't understand, Pierre,' she says. 'Please, tell me what's going on. I mean, Hélène's things? Her beautiful things in *my* shop?'

'Your daughter and my nephew – and a few of their friends – worked day and night to fix up the shop,' Mr LeBoeff says. (I notice that he hasn't let go of her hand.) 'They put their hearts and souls into it. Andy has many ideas about how to make it prosperous. Part of which will involve my old theatre.' He points to the space that the curtain is covering – where the wall we knocked down once stood.

My voice trembles slightly as I explain the 'concept' of *The Polka Dot Shop*. How we'll sell a mixture of top-end vintage fashion, consignment, and new clothing by young designers. 'We want to create a "destination",' I say, using the fashion professor's word. 'With something for everyone who loves fashion. Classic, modern, timeless, fun.'

'But . . .' Mum says, and I'm alarmed to see tears trickling down her cheeks, 'how can we possibly afford all this?'

Mr LeBoeff takes a clean tissue from his pocket and hands it to her. He tells her about how we've sold some of his wife's things to make money to fix up the shop.

'In truth, the idea was a painful one for me to accept,' he says. 'But I think it is for the best. We must look to the future.' He smiles at her.

Thomas gives me a wide-eyed look of surprise. 'No idea,' I mouth back silently.

'Which is what Andy and Thomas have been doing,' Mr LeBoeff adds.

'And we've had lots of free help,' I say, jumping in. 'My friends, and Jolanta, and her boyfriend.'

'Jolanta? She's involved too?' Mum's tears come faster now. 'I . . . I'm so . . .'

'Yes, Eliza,' a voice comes from the back of the shop. I've almost forgotten the fact that I'd called Jolanta last night and told her about the 'unveiling' to Mum. 'I hope that's OK.'

'Oh, Jolanta!' Mum rushes over and gives her a hug. 'It's so good to see you.' I don't even feel jealous (OK – maybe a little). But I'm glad that Mum's happy to see her.

'It's good to be here,' Jolanta says. 'I love the

shop. And I want it to do well. I think – I hope – that Andy has found a way.' She looks over at me and gives me a little smile. There's not even a trace of smugness on her face (OK – maybe a little).

Mum and Jolanta separate (finally). We all watch in silence as Mum walks around the shop, taking everything in. It seems to take for ever.

'Where did the idea for the polka dots come from?' she says finally.

I look at Thomas. He looks at me. I feel my stomach plummet.

'Um, remember the white bag?' I look at the walls, the floor, anywhere other than at Mum – or Mr LeBoeff. 'It was left on the doorstep by the dry-cleaner. I gave everything back to Thomas. Except for one thing. A dress by Chanel. Black with white polka dots and a full skirt.'

'That dress,' Mr LeBoeff says. 'I remember it.'

I have to look at him then. He seems lost in his own world. 'She got it from a friend,' he says. 'An old woman she knew who modelled the dress back in the fifties. It was lovely and sparkly, and Hélène looked so . . .' He shakes his head, unable to continue.

'I'm sorry that I took it,' I say. 'I sold it on eBay without your permission.'

'Andy!' Mum looks shocked. 'You didn't.'

I hang my head. This is not how I wanted the day to go.

Thomas comes up and stands at my side. 'Andy told me about it,' he says, taking in both his uncle and my mum. 'I told her to send it to the buyer and keep the money. It was my mistake that it got left on the doorstep. Andy didn't know where the dress came from when she listed it.'

'And we used the money to buy paint for the shop,' I say, knowing that I'm probably digging myself into a deeper hole. At Stevie's house the other night, I'd emailed the buyer of the dress asking if maybe I could buy it back. I haven't had a response to my message.

'I'm so sorry, Pierre,' Mum says to Mr LeBoeff. 'This must be very hard for you.'

He smiles at Mum, and rests a hand lightly on her arm. 'Thomas and Andy did what they thought was best. They might not have got everything right, but then, who does? Let us not be too hard on them.'

I kind of feel like Mum's forgotten that I'm there. She looks at Pierre LeBoeff and he looks at her. Thomas, still standing next to me, nudges me with his elbow.

'Of course,' Mum says, finally coming back to her senses. 'It's all just a lot to take in.'

'But do you . . . like it?' I say. I hold my breath. This is it – everything we've worked towards. I'm proud of what we've done, but at the end of the day, we need Mum to help make this work.

She turns towards me and for a second I can see her whole life in her eyes. Her sadness over my dad's death, her struggles with the business, her love of the former *Eliza's Emporium*, her efforts to be a good mum to me, even though she was suffering from depression. And now I see something else there too. Maybe I'm imagining it, but it looks like . . . hope.

'Oh, Andy . . .' is all she says. She opens her arms and enfolds me into them. Her tears dampen my cheek.

I hold her tightly, feeling the love and warmth between us. And I know that whatever happens, we'll be in it together.

36

A WISH COME TRUE

I feel like I'm walking on air. Mum is in on the secret and she's on board — sort of. Naturally, she has her own ideas. For one thing (and she's right about this, I know) she wants to pay Mr LeBoeff back all the money for the clothing and the shop fittings. He protests, but being the perfect French gentleman, he lets her 'win'. They go together for a coffee and manage to work something out — I don't know the details exactly, but it involves him owning part of the shop as a 'silent partner' or something, until she makes enough to buy him out. I didn't realize before that Mum knew about Hélène and her things, but I guess they've been neighbours for so long that it makes sense. When she comes back from meeting him, she has an awful lot of colour in her cheeks. 'Pierre is such a lovely man!' is all I can get out of her.

The other thing that she insists on is going through all the old clothes we culled and put in the basement of the theatre. When she appears upstairs with several bin bags full of the stock we discarded, I have a few tense moments. But luckily, Jolanta is on hand to sort us out. We rely on her to make the final decision. (Mostly she sides with me – except for the denim, that is!)

Mum also goes on her own to the fashion school and meets the designers who have signed up to rent studio space. Naturally, they all love her and her love of clothes, and she loves them, so that works out OK. But there's one thing that Mum does that really surprises me. She calls up a TV station and tells them all about our project. There's a lady who does shows on 'revitalizing the high street' and she loves the idea of a shop being transformed by a thirteen-year-old. They decide to send a film crew to cover our grand opening.

But for me, the best thing is that a few days after Mum comes back, I finally get a reply to my message from the buyer of the polka-dot dress. Apparently, she loved the dress and wore it to some kind of fifties ball. But she's happy to sell it back to me for the price she bought it for. Which is really great – except I don't have the money. This time, instead of going behind Mum's back, I go straight to her. I get another earful – how I shouldn't have taken it without her permission, and how Thomas and I should have checked with 'Pierre'. She gives me a lecture on how we need to tell each other the truth; be a team—

'Yeah, Mum, I know. And I'm sorry. But what should I do now?'

'Well, Andy, to be honest, I'm dying to see this polka-dot dress. I've applied for a bank loan to cover some of our costs, and I should get the money on Friday. Can it wait until then?'

'Yeah, perfect,' I say. I can't wait to tell the others. It's all coming together – but there's still so much to do. With everything that's happening, I feel exited and scared and bubbly and a little sick all at the same time. But then, I'm getting kind of used to that – ever since I met Thomas.

Thomas . . .

As much as my wishes are coming true about the shop, when I lie awake at night, there's a knot in my chest. I don't want to admit the reason for it, but ever since Mum came back, it feels like he's avoiding me. I miss the times we had together before the others got involved – painting, dancing, and always in the back of my mind, the white x he traced on my cheek.

Now, it's like the only times I ever see him are when I'm over at Stevie's house – he seems to be there a lot helping her with her walking. Which is great – it really is. I know she appreciates his help, and I'm glad that they're such good friends. But sometimes, I have this little niggle . . . (OK – sometimes I wish it was still just him and me.)

A week after Mum's return, I go over to Stevie's house on a night I know Thomas is working. I just feel like I need to clear the air, hang out with Stevie on her own. I also really miss the times I had with my friends before I got so busy with the shop.

When I get there, Stevie's mum tells me that she's not home – she's having an extra session with the physio because the walking is putting a strain on her lower back. 'Is she going to be OK?' I say, feeling worried for my friend.

Stevie's mum gives me a brittle smile. 'It's hard on her body,' she says. 'But it's something she really wants – so she's going to do it. She wants to be like you, Andy.'

'No!' I can feel myself blushing. How can Stevie, of all people, want to be like me?

'All the work you've been doing at the shop

has inspired her. So good on you.'

'Thanks.' When she says it, I feel proud, but it also makes me realize how much I've been neglecting my friends and their goals. Carrie – she had a plan too, something she wanted to do for the school project, and for herself. She wanted to get fit and lose weight. I wonder though whether she ought to be so obsessed with those things. I mean, it's good to be healthy, but how much of Carrie's plan to transform her life is mostly to please her dad?

I decide to walk over to her house and see if she's around. When I get there and knock on the door, I have to wait a whole minute and I start thinking that she's not home, when suddenly she answers the door. She's wearing a stripy apron and her hands are dusty with flour. 'Andy!' she says, looking surprised to see me. 'Come in – I'm just about to start baking. Cinnamon scones.' Her face seems to light up. 'I've joined this new online cooking club. Some girl is writing a blog and posting all these really cool recipes. I wanted to try one.'

'That's great,' I say, somewhat warily. It's none of my business but surely making (and eating) scones doesn't exactly square with her goal of getting fit.

Carrie seems to pick up on my hesitation. 'I know, I know . . .' she says. 'I'm not supposed to eat cakes and stuff. But I've been reading up on how to eat better. I've found out that the worst thing is processed foods – frozen pizzas, fish fingers – I'm cutting all that stuff out. I want to learn to cook home-made things – healthy stuff as well as sweets.'

'That sounds good,' I say. Whatever she's doing, there's something different about her – in a good way. I can't quite put my finger on what it is.

She catches me looking at her. Her face – she has high cheekbones and really nice skin. Her eyes are a bright and sunny shade of cornflower blue. She's really pretty – and I don't think I ever noticed it before. 'What?' she says.

'You look really good,' I say, smiling.

She frowns, like she's trying to suss out whether or not I'm lying.

'I haven't lost weight,' she says. 'I mean, not very much anyway. But even so, I've managed to do the one thing I really needed to.'

'What's that?'

I sit down at the kitchen table and she pours us both a glass of apple juice, then says, 'I told my dad last night that I'm not doing boot camp any more.'

'Really?'

'Yeah. I did. He didn't take it well at first, but I think he's coming around.'

'What did you say to him?'

She shrugs. 'I told him the truth. That it was making me feel even worse about myself. Like because I'm fat, there's something wrong with me as a person.'

'That's awful, Carrie. There's nothing wrong with you. You're great.'

She smiles, and begins setting out the ingredients for the scones: flour, water, a mixing bowl, a wooden spoon. 'I told him how they were like "get down and give me twenty, you lazy slug", or "eat cake – run two extra miles". And they had all these slogans like "a moment on the lips, a lifetime on the hips", and "couch potatoes finish last". It was just – you know – like, really demoralizing.'

'Horrible.'

'It was. So I talked to the school nurse. She agreed with me that it wasn't helping – not in the way I need, anyway. So she found me a group – you know, for therapy.'

'Therapy? But you don't need that!'

'It's for teenagers who have problems – some with weight, some with other things like their parents, or anger and stuff – and they want to feel better about themselves. It meets once a week. I've been once. And it was good.' She laughs. 'I mean, I thought *I* had issues, but you should see the others!'

'I bet.'

She measures out the flour on the scales. 'Anyway, so Dad says we can do something else – I'm not sure what, though he did mention cycling.' She wrinkles her nose. 'I'm not going to get out of this fitness thing that easily.'

'No,' I laugh. 'I guess not.'

'And what do you think of the clothes? When you were helping Jolanta with the studio rooms the other night, I helped your mum sort through a new bag of consignment stuff. She picked them out for me – as "payment" for helping out.'

Because she's wearing an apron, I hadn't noticed, but now I do. She's wearing a fitted blue T-shirt with a V-neck. Not her usual giant man-style sweatshirt. And instead of trainers, she's wearing a neat pair of black leather loafers with a low heel. It makes her look taller, slimmer and much more confident. 'The top is from New Look,' she says proudly.

'You look great, Carrie. I knew something was different about you. It's fab, really really fab!'

Her cheeks grow pink. 'Thanks, Andy,' she says.

'You inspired me – with all your hard work and ideas. I hope the shop is a big success.'

I give her a big hug. 'I'm so proud of you.'

'Thanks. Um, Andy . . .'

'Yeah?'

'Do you want to help me with the scones?'

'But I've never baked anything in my life.'

'Have you ever fixed up a shop before now?'

'Well . . . no.'

She grins. 'I guess there's a first time for everything.' She hands me the wooden spoon and pours the flour into the mixing bowl.

37

TO HAVE LOVED AND LOST . . .

I feel so proud of Carrie – and Stevie – and myself, I guess. The next day at school, Stevie looks pale and I can tell that she's in a lot of pain with her back. 'I may not be a rocket scientist like you,' I say, 'but even I can see that you need to take it a little slower.'

Her eyes cloud with tears. 'But I was making such good progress. I wanted to be able to walk again before Thomas—' She breaks off suddenly.

'Thomas?' I say slowly. 'What does he have to do with it?'

'Nothing.' She shakes her head. 'I meant before the grand opening.'

'Oh.'

Stevie may be many things, but she's not a good liar. She's hiding something — and I have a pretty good idea what it is. My heart feels like an egg that's been tapped on the edge of a frying pan, ready to crack in two.

Stevie and Thomas, Thomas and Stevie. I go over and over it in my head as I walk to the shop after school. For a while now I've had this little niggle, a thought that's sprouted in my head like a seed. But I didn't want to acknowledge that it might be true. Stevie's smart and funny and pretty in a geek girl kind of way. I should feel happy for her. I mean, it's not like she set out to steal Thomas from me. It's not like I have any claim on him to begin with — other than a slow dance and a white x. Besides, he's fourteen — a whole year older than me, and at least six months older than Stevie. It's not like he'd want someone like me for a girl-friend, and if he and Stevie . . . well, it's none of my business. I'll just try to be happy for them, and try not to let them see how much it hurts.

I get to *The Polka Dot Shop* and stand in front of the window. Until the grand opening, the window is covered by white canvas. I try to imag-ine what it will look like. The display area has been painted all white, with a black polka-dot border. In the centre, we'll have a white dress form with the polka-dot dress (I haven't received it back from the buyer, though apparently it's in the post). Everything will be sleek, modern and classy. There will be no more stained wedding dresses, hula skirts or mannequins painted like scary clowns. Even 'Amelie' has been given a makeover – a real wig instead of painted-on hair. She'll be on display inside the door wearing a shimmering ivory beaded gown by Valentino that will be one of our key display pieces.

I peer through the panes of glass in the shop door. Mum and Jolanta are inside, chatting and sorting through some of the consignment pieces – just like old times. I'll have to go through whatever they choose and cull some of it – that much I know. While the shop is officially closed until the relaunch, we've done a lot of advertising of the new consignment operation. Lots of people have dropped things off that they're hoping we'll sell and they'll get a percentage. A few days ago, Ms Cartwright came by to see what we've been up to, and I showed her the things I'd put aside for her. (Shoes and clothing only – no more bras or 'pre-owned' underwear!) I thought she was going to faint when she saw some of Hélène's things that were hanging on the racks. She came back the next day with three giant bags of clothing from before and after her gender reassignment.

'I don't have the money to buy many nice new things,' she'd said, 'but if I sell some of my clothes, maybe I'll be able to buy some of your fabulous new stock!' She'd been drawn to a rack of some of Hélène's more colourful pieces – a red silk corset dress with a puffy tulle underskirt, a backless beaded ballgown in emerald crepe, a micro minidress in a Mondrian print. (They'll have to be altered to fit her, and I have no idea where she's planning to wear them, but I'm sure her students will have plenty to talk about.)

Now, part of me is tempted to go inside and help out Mum and Jolanta – try to enjoy going through the new stock; try and forget about this hurt inside me. But I know that I'm going to need to face it eventually. Without consciously thinking about where I'm going, I walk around to the back of the parade of shops, and past the open door of Mum's shop. I make my way to the small door one building over – the old theatre. It's the one place I can think of where I can have some space – some time alone to clear my head.

I go into the corridor and walk up to the black velvet curtain that separates the old dressing rooms – the soon-to-be studios – from the main area. I step inside the main space of the theatre, breathing in the smell of fresh paint and newly varnished wood. The curtain separating the theatre from Mum's shop has been drawn and I can barely hear the sound of muffled voices.

Just being in that vast white space makes me feel instantly calmer. I turn around slowly in a circle. I want to surround myself in the feeling of newness before the shop opens to the public. I want to enjoy this thing I've helped create while it's still mine.

But when I come round to face the stage, I realize that I'm not alone. Thomas is lying down on the stage, his head resting in his hands, just like once before when I came upon him. The radio is next to him, but it's turned off. He's staring up at the ceiling, not moving.

In an instant, the options flash before me. Tiptoe out and leave him alone; or should I stay and talk to him? My stomach takes a dive. What if he's waiting for Stevie?

Either way, I have to know.

'Thomas?' I say quietly. 'Is it OK if I come in?'

He swivels towards me. If he's surprised that it's me instead of . . . anyone else, he doesn't show it. And when he smiles at me, my insides melt like butter. 'Andy,' he says. 'Long time no see.'

I walk over to the stage and sit on the edge. 'I thought you were at work.'

'Were you hoping to have the place to yourself?'

I laugh at his insightfulness. 'Yes, I was, but you being here – well, that's OK too. You know – like old times.'

'Yeah, it is. And I'm glad you're here.'

I take a breath. 'You don't have to say that. I guess you were hoping that it was Stevie instead of me.'

He gives me a puzzled glance. 'Stevie? Why?'

'You two seem very close.'

'Well, we are, I guess. I'm helping her with the walking. She's your friend – my friend too, I think. She wants to be able to do the same things that you and Carrie can do.'

I give a little laugh. 'Don't worry. I totally understand what you see in her. She's smart and funny and sweet.'

He scrambles up on to his elbow, looking surprised. 'What are you trying to say?'

Unconsciously, my hand goes to my cheek. The one where X marked the spot. Once. A long time ago . . .

I shrug. 'Just that I'm OK with it.'

'Hmm.' He lies back again. For a long time, he's

silent. That in itself seems like confirmation.

'I love this place,' he says finally.

I'm so preoccupied with my own thoughts that I barely realize that we're not talking about Stevie any more.

'From the moment I came in here – when it was practically a ruin. There was something about it that spoke to me, if that makes sense.'

'I . . . think so.'

He swings up and sits at the edge of the stage, his legs dangling over. As much as I'm happy finally to be alone with him again – like in the early days when we were painting the theatre – I'm a little bit scared too. Scared of the way he makes me feel. I sit down next to him – within arm's reach, but with a space between us. I stare out at the serene white space of the theatre, but inside, butterflies tickle my stomach.

'I've got something to tell you, Andy.'

I don't move – don't look at him; don't even breathe. No one ever says those words if they've got something good to say.

'What?' I say hesitantly.

'I didn't want to tell you before, but there's another reason I wanted to get the theatre sorted for my uncle.'

'So that it looked good for the estate agents?' I

try to make a joke but it falls flat.

'No.' I feel his hand inch towards mine. 'It's not that.' He traces a line down the top of my hand, to the tip of my finger. My skin feels like it's sparkling.

'What then?'

'It's because I'm leaving,' he says.

'Leaving? What do you mean?'

He turns to face me, still keeping hold of my hand.

'I'm moving to Paris. I'm going to finish the term out there so I can settle in to the new school. I didn't want to tell you . . .'

My mind is a whirlwind of confusion and hurt. He's not interested in Stevie – or any of us. He's leaving. Going away. I fight back the urge to grab my hand away, stand up, run off. I want to do those things – anything to escape the cracks that I can feel forming in my heart.

But instead I sit there, paralysed, gripping his hand in mine and not wanting to let go.

'Why?' I say finally.

'It was my uncle's suggestion. He says I should finish school in Paris. I'll have a better chance of getting into uni there if I do. For now, I'm going to live with his brother, my Uncle Jules and his wife. They've got a really big apartment on the Left Bank.'

'That makes sense . . . I guess.' I try to keep my voice steady. 'And is your uncle going too?'

'He hasn't decided yet. He has a friend who's offered him a job managing a restaurant – like he used to do. It was his passion before my aunt died. But he's not sure yet if he wants to sell the chippie.' He lowers his voice. 'And, as I'm sure you've noticed, there might be another reason he wants to stay.'

I laugh, but my heart's not in it. 'Yeah, I've noticed. Mum and your uncle. It's a little weird, but kind of nice for them too.'

'I agree,' Thomas says. 'Anyway, he'll probably come with me to Paris for a little while and decide what he wants to do.'

A swell of pain rises up in my chest. Just like I knew that for Mum and me, revamping the shop was the right thing to do, I know equally that Thomas and his uncle need to do the right thing for them.

'But what about *The Polka Dot Shop*?' My voice cracks. 'What about me?'

'Oh, Andy . . .' Thomas swallows hard. 'I'm going to miss all of this – so much. Your friends, this place. But most of all . . . you.' He squeezes my hand. 'You, Andy.'

When I see a tear rolling down his cheek, I

can't hold back any longer. My eyes erupt like a leaking water fountain. And at that moment, I would give anything – all the vintage designer clothing; a shopping trip to Westfield; a whole wardrobe from Topshop – to have him stay. Except that would be wrong.

I lean over and dry the tear with my finger. 'Thomas – I'm absolutely sure you're doing the right thing. Go to Paris – that's where you should be. You're going to make a fantastic architect.'

His smile is like the sun bursting through rain-clouds. 'I'll come back to visit – I promise. I'm definitely going to be here for the grand opening.'

'You'd better,' I say. 'I'm going to need some help setting up the catwalk.'

'And you can come visit me too,' he says. 'In Paris. The fashion capital of Europe.'

'I'd like to,' I say sadly. 'But for me, the fashion capital is right here.' I gesture around me. 'Or at least, some day it will be.'

He laughs. 'Of that I have no doubt.'

We sit there holding hands. I want to stay like that for ever – lock the pain outside the door, and out of my life. But I know that's impossible.

'Thomas?' A voice filters into the theatre – it's Mr LeBoeff.

'Coming,' he calls back. He lets go of my hand

and stands up.

I stand up too. He turns to me, and I try to memorize his face. There's a shyness about him all of a sudden that I've rarely seen.

And before I can even think about what I'm doing, I reach out and put my arms around his neck. The world shrinks to a bubble around us. My lips brush his, and we hold each other close. I close my eyes to blink back the tears.

When I open them again, he's gone.

38

ENDINGS AND BEGINNINGS

'It's not fair,' Carrie says. 'We haven't even had the grand opening yet.' We're sitting at the back of Mum's shop two days later, making price tags. I've broken the news about Thomas. Stevie knew already – that's what she meant by wanting to walk before he left. But even she had no idea how soon it was going to happen.

'I guess Andy's attitude of getting on with things inspired them too,' Stevie says, sounding falsely cheerful. 'Why wait? Mr LeBoeff isn't getting any younger. They should move back to Paris if that's what they want.'

'It just won't be the same without him,' Carrie says.

'No, it won't,' I say, swallowing hard. 'But Stevie's right. They've got a good opportunity – they should take it.'

I've thought a lot about Mr LeBoeff over the last few days – probably to keep my mind off . . . someone else. I've thought about how generous he's been in helping me and Mum by investing in the shop, when he could have just sold the theatre for a gym and left it at that. I've thought about how he came here to help his wife, and when she died, the dream died with her. He could have gone back to Paris at that time, but he stayed. I guess at first he wanted to be close to her memory. But as time went on, it just became too hard to change. I don't know if he felt depressed himself, or if he was just in a rut. But either way, it took Thomas and me – our help in clearing out the old to make room for the new – that helped him move on too. Just like with Mum and her shop.

I guess if I've learned one thing from the last few months, it's to try not to be afraid to change things that aren't working. Without warning, my eyes fill with tears. Carrie's right – it's not fair. With Thomas here, things *were* working.

'Hey,' Carrie says, noticing that I'm upset. 'He'll be back – I mean, they own part of the shop, don't they? I'm sure Thomas will want to keep an eye on their investment.'

I smile. 'You're right, I'm sure he will. Especially since I'm not sure his uncle is going anywhere.' I've told them my suspicions about Mum and Mr LeBoeff. Stevie was surprised, but Carrie not so much. In any case, we'll all have to wait and see.

'And who knows?' Stevie says. 'Maybe some day you'll visit Thomas in Paris. Hey, maybe we'll all go.' She smiles. 'I can picture the three of us, *walking* through the station to get the Eurostar.'

'Yeah!' Carrie says. 'I've always wanted to go to Paris. I mean, just imagine . . .'

I nod, allowing myself to be swept up in their enthusiasm. Paris. Who knows? They have more than just good schools for architecture in Paris. And Mum is always banging on about me going to uni. But for now . . . that's a long way off. I've got a shop to open, a mum to manage, and Ms Cartwright wants us to write a whole report on our 'transformation' for her class. Because it seems that more people in the school than just us took the project seriously.

One boy sent a short story he wrote to a BBC contest, and two other girls are organizing a charity bake-off at school to raise money for refugees. Another girl is training to run a 5k race, another boy is earning pocket money by running errands for elderly people in his neighbourhood. The class is buzzing with ideas, and even if we have to write a report, it's still been worth it. Ms Cartwright said that Carrie could change her goal – from losing six kilos to learning how to cook healthy food. And Stevie . . . well, her goal was always going to be ambitious to do in one term. I can see from the dark circles under her eyes that she's not sleeping well and is still in pain, but she's refusing to give up. That in itself is inspiring.

'Paris would be fun,' I say, 'but right now, I'm glad I'm here – I mean, there's so much to do before we open—'

The bell tinkles on the door at the front of the shop. I go through the curtain from the back to see who's there. Mum goes to open the door – even though we're not officially open yet, lots of people have seen our advertisements and are bringing clothing by for us to take 'on consignment'. She greets a middle-aged woman wearing a baggy cardigan, a tweed skirt and sensible shoes. The woman is carrying two huge 'bags for life' that are brimming with clothing. I eye them, wondering if they're filled with trash or treasure.

'Come right this way, Mrs Sandborn,' Mum is saying. She ushers the woman over to the new counter with the till. 'Now, if you want to leave the bag, I can go through it and make sure everything gets labelled properly for sale. We've got a new system, you see.'

I come up to them. 'Mum, actually, I'll go through it now if you like.' I turn to the woman. 'We've got a new system, as Eliza was saying. I'm afraid we're only taking on designer labels at the moment.' I go quickly through the clothing at the top of the bag. It's mostly faded old T-shirts and floral print skirts. And down a few layers, I get to the *pièce de resistance* – a stack of shiny polyester pants. With a smile, I hand the bag back to the woman.

'Sorry to waste your time,' I say. 'For your convenience, we've put a charity collection bin out the back in the alleyway.'

The woman looks at me in shock. I stand up straight – I'm at least three inches taller than she is. Beside me, Mum looks like she wants to dig a hole in the ground and crawl inside.

Then, to my surprise, the woman starts to laugh. 'Quite right,' she says. 'And fair enough. I was having a clear-out, and didn't know what to do with most of it. I thought of your mum's shop. But next time, I'll think twice.' She points to the second bag. 'You might be interested in that one, though. I've got a couple of nice suits from Joseph.'

'That's great,' I say. 'I'll definitely have a look.'

'I'm sorry ...' Mum begins. 'It's a new thing ...'

The woman holds up her hand. 'If you're now such sticklers for quality, I might have a little look around. I'm looking for a dress to wear for my niece's wedding. And I love what you've done with the place. It looks really high-end. And I can actually see the clothing that's for sale.'

'Oh, of course.' Mum ushers the woman over to a rack of dresses. 'We do have some lovely things. You are very welcome to take a look.'

Smiling to myself, I go through the second bag and 'rescue' the two Joseph suits, a dress from Whistles and a woollen skirt from Hobbs. I assign Mrs Sandborn a customer number in my consignment filing system, and write her number on the back of the price tag for the item. That way, when the item sells, she'll be able to get her sixty per cent. In store credit.

I glance over to where Mum is showing her some of the things we have hanging on the rack from La Belle Hélène's collection. Mrs Sandborn takes a plain silk crepe dress in seafoam green off the rack and holds it up to her neck. It's about six sizes too small for her, but the colour brings out the green of her eyes.

'This is exquisite,' she says. 'But I don't think I could get more than one leg into it.'

I leave the till and come up to them. 'This dress really suits you. It would be perfect, wouldn't it? If you really love it, then one of the services we will be offering at *The Polka Dot Shop* is a customized design and dressmaking service. I can have Jolanta, our designer, take your measurements, and she can create something similar just for you. Would you like me to make you an appointment?'

'I . . . don't know.' The woman looks at me, then at Mum, then at the dress. 'I do love it. What would it cost?'

Mum opens her mouth to speak but I cut her off.

'For a dress similar to this in crepe-backed satin, it would be one hundred and eighty pounds plus VAT. That's much less than you would pay on the high street for something of this quality, and it would be made to measure.'

The woman looks at the dress, then only at me. 'And when would it be ready?'

'When do you need it by?'

We discuss the details, booking her in for an appointment with Jolanta, and eventually Mrs Sandborn leaves me a forty per cent deposit on the dress, and leaves the shop with the items we're not taking for consignment. On the way out she thanks me and Mum – who's still looking like a deer in the headlights. But what makes me happiest is that the woman never once asks me how old I am, and I get the feeling that it never even crossed her mind.

As soon as the door closes, Mum sinks down on the stool by the till. I'm aware also that Stevie and Carrie have come in from the back, and must have seen some of it too – because they start applauding.

'Well done,' Carrie says. 'That was brilliant. You're not even officially open yet and you've made a sale!'

'Yeah,' Stevie says. 'And it's good that you remembered about the VAT.'

'I think I'm going to have a heart attack,' Mum says.

It's only then that I notice how fast my own heart is beating from the adrenaline of making a sale. It's kind of like the rush I get when I find something exciting in one of the consignment lots (especially things that are new and still have the tags on!) Only, it's better than that. Because clothing seasons come and go, but what I've done – and what I've learned – will last.

'We'll get there, Mum,' I say. 'Remember, it can be hard to have a go at something new.'

'Well . . . you certainly have made me proud, Andy. And happy.'

Hearing this, I feel a prickle of tears. I'm not kidding myself that it's going to be easy to make our new venture work, but I know that it's given Mum and me a new lease of life. For right now, that's enough.

'That's good, Mum,' I say. 'Now, I'd better go and find Jolanta and tell her about the appointment. Wanna come?' I smile at Stevie and Carrie.

'Sure.'

My two friends come up the aisle in the shop. I've made sure that the clothing racks are spaced wide enough apart so that wheelchairs and prams can get through easily. It's interesting how having fewer things stuffed on the racks has made the shop seem much bigger. We go through the arch that leads to the theatre, and the designer studios in the back.

As soon as I step into the main room, I miss Thomas. The room itself is still undergoing a transformation – the displays of Hélène's best pieces that will eventually go to a museum, and the catwalk that's being built out from the stage like a long pier in a calm white ocean. Some of

Hélène's things are hanging from the racks, still wrapped in their protective bags. I can hear the faint sound of a radio coming from Jolanta's studio at the back.

And at that moment, as much as I'm aware of Thomas's absence, I feel something else too — something strange, but powerful. Stevie stops her wheelchair in the centre of the room and looks at Carrie, then at me. Carrie's mouth opens and closes. Whatever it is, they feel it too.

It's almost like there's another presence in the room, the way I felt when Thomas and I danced in this place that holds so many memories of wartime joys and sorrows. But this time, I can almost imagine that La Belle Hélène is here herself, in spirit, along with the designers who made her their muse. And I know that I'm part of something larger than myself. Something timeless and enduring.

'Thank you,' I whisper into the ether. 'Thank you so much.'

EPILOGUE
THE GRAND OPENING
SIX WEEKS LATER

On the morning of the grand opening, sunlight streams in through a gap in the curtains, and for a second I worry that I've overslept. I'm out of bed and dressed in black jeans and a black *The Polka Dot Shop* T-shirt before I realize that it's only six a.m.! I go to the window, open it and take a few deep breaths of warm spring air. The trees outside have gone from blossom to green, and Easter is on its way. All in the time that Thomas has been gone. Sometimes it's felt like for ever, sometimes like only a few days. We've emailed and Skyped a few times, and I know that he's trying really hard to keep in touch and is planning to come back for the grand opening. But I also know that he's got a new life now – meeting new people, going to a new school. I've kept myself busy too with school (Mum says she'll only let me help out at the shop if my schoolwork doesn't suffer, so I'm trying extra hard). At the shop I've also been helping the designers settle in to their studio space, getting the whole consignment process up and running, and selling endless things on eBay. But even with so much going on, little things remind me of how much I miss him.

I trace the phantom outline of a white x on my cheek. Will he come today, as promised? Or will it all be too much of an effort? Either way, I need to keep a clear head so that I can get on with the million tasks I need to do before this afternoon. Even though I've been working flat out for weeks and I'm pretty sure everything is ready, I plan to use every second to make things perfect.

Mum is already in the kitchen when I go downstairs. She's made me a mug of hot chocolate, and a plate of eggs and soldiers. Though I feel sick with nerves, today of all days I know I need to keep my strength up.

'You look great, Mum,' I say as she brings the food over. She really does. She's wearing our logo T-shirt and a floaty chiffon maxi skirt in a zebra print (I'm pretty sure I put it in a bin bag, but then she 'rescued' it). Her wrists are covered with her signature bangles, and she's got a necklace of some kind of black-and-white seeds. I'm glad that despite all the changes we've made, Mum still has her own unique 'vintage' style. I guess I've learned that not everyone has to like the same things.

'Thanks – you too.' Mum looks at my prim black outfit. 'You look very grown-up, Andy.'

'Do I?'

'Yes. It's not just the clothes. It's everything you've done. You're different somehow.'

I choke back a tear. 'I think we both are.'

She takes my hand and squeezes it. 'Try to enjoy today,' she says. 'You deserve it.'

'Thanks, Mum.' I squeeze her hand back. 'You too. And it's going to be great – I just know it.'

And I do know it . . . but I still feel nervous.

After breakfast, I leave to go to the theatre. Mr LeBoeff knows some local caterers and is working with them to prepare lots of nice canapés for the launch. He's also making some miniature baskets of his to-die-for fish and chips. They're due to start setting up the food around noon. The same time the models are due to arrive. We got the names of the models from Jolanta's fashion school

– all of them are looking to get catwalk experience and some portfolio shots, so they're doing it for free.

We've got a few other freebies as well. Jolanta has another friend who's a photography student. He's coming to photograph the event (in return for a case of beer). Stevie has put together a website for the shop, and it's going to be my responsibility to keep it up to date with events, photos and special promotions. Mum's also had a lesson in computers – she's now in charge of our eBay shop where she'll list special pieces that come into *The Polka Dot Shop*. As manager of the business, she'll have her work cut out for her keeping on top of everything in real time and cyberspace. But at least now she's got Jolanta back, and if we're really successful, maybe she'll be able to hire another assistant so that she has more time to 'talk fashion' with the customers. I know that Mum's still taking her tablets – she says she has to be on them for at least a year. But she seems so much brighter – because of what's happening with the shop; and also because we're getting along so much better. Whether we succeed or fail, that's worth everything to me.

The front door of the shop is closed and the window is still covered over. I enter through the back. The front of the shop has racks of the consignment clothing for sale, and some new designer pieces by the fashion students. Eventually, we plan to turn the part of the space that was *Eliza's Emporium* into a café and fashion bookshop, and have the theatre as the shop floor for the clothing. Right now, though, the theatre stage has been turned into a huge catwalk, with chairs on either side set up for the grand opening fashion show.

The rest of the theatre is being used to showcase some of La Belle Hélène's pieces — almost like a museum of fashion. Of course, almost everything's for sale — but even I find some of the prices a little bit shocking. Jolanta's professor, though, has assured us that the clothing is special and worth every penny.

I walk to the window at the front of the shop. The centrepiece is a plain white dress form with the black-and-white polka-dot dress by Chanel, accessorized with a single strand of pearls and a black patent leather handbag and shoes. It already looks perfect, but I plump out the skirt so that the glitter tulle in the underskirt sparkles in the new shop lighting. The plan is that after the shop is unveiled to the public, the dress will come out of the window, and one of the models will wear it in the fashion show.

I spend an hour or so just checking on things – that the tables are set up for the caterers, the speakers are plugged in, and that the sound and light system for the fashion show (courtesy of another friend of Jolanta) is plugged in. I also log into the laptop where we've set up all our online profiles. There's been a lot of traffic on Twitter about the grand opening, and there are seven fashion bloggers and vloggers scheduled to attend our event (two of them are teen bloggers). Carrie also got some people from her online cooking club to say they'll come, and they're bringing a great big celebration cake.

In other words, while everything is sorted, there are a lot of moving parts. I've done what I can to put things in motion. Now I can only cross my fingers and hope . . .

Over the next few hours, it's chaos as people begin to arrive – caterers, models, the sound and light crew, and the bloggers and journalists. Mum is in her element 'talking vintage' with customers old and new. One of the new customers is the woman from London who bought the polka-dot dress and sold it back to me. When I sent her the invite, she was very keen to come and see what else is for sale from Hélène's collection.

As I'm showing some of the bloggers around the shop, there's a commotion outside as several large vans arrive with the film crew sent to cover our grand opening for their show about revitalizing local high streets. They confirm that the woman from TV who revitalizes high-street shops will be on hand to witness the makeover of *Eliza's Emporium* into *The Polka Dot Shop*. Mr LeBoeff and Aunt Linda – who has come down from the Lakes for the opening – direct the vans to park behind the shop. Carrie, Stevie and I are on hand to help them unload their equipment, find the electrical outlets, point the way to the toilets, and generally make sure that the crew is fed and watered.

The hours fly by and pretty soon it's almost two o'clock. Outside, there are people milling about on the pavement waiting for the doors to *The Polka Dot Shop* to open and the window to be unveiled for the first time – waiting to come and experience the newest shopping 'destination'. I spot Ms Cartwright wearing the Mondrian print dress that she bought and had altered, and Stevie's parents and Carrie's dad. I feel a little jolt of pride when I see Chloe, Olivia and a few other members of the 'fashion police' queuing up by the door.

At two o'clock exactly, I stand at the door next to Mum. Behind us, Mr LeBoeff is there, his solid presence comforting in all the chaos.

Mum gives my hand a quick squeeze. 'OK – it's time,' she says.

My fingers feel jittery as I unlock the door. A black-and-white ribbon is stretched across the doorframe. Mr LeBoeff hands Mum a pair of scissors. The crowd gathers, ready to come inside. Mum cuts the ribbon and it falls away. From inside, Jolanta pulls the canvas down from the window. The polka-dot dress is classic and perfect, and the window looks just like I'd imagined. People begin snapping photos of it with their phones as they queue to get into the shop.

'Welcome,' Mum says, ushering in the first customers.

The next hour is a blur of people – customers looking at the clothing, asking questions, trying things on. The fashion bloggers take photos of the shop, me, Mum, Hélène's collection. The till rings constantly as the sales begin. There are queues at the fitting rooms, and the young designers are hovering around talking about their work. The TV camera crew conducts a few interviews. Stevie and Carrie seem to have disappeared – I can't find them anywhere.

And Thomas. There's no Thomas.

I take a breath trying to steel myself against the hurt I feel inside. He's not coming. It was too much to hope for. I understand that now. Paris is a long way away. I have to accept it and move on. I just have to!

Eventually, Mum comes and finds me. I think she guesses how I'm feeling, because she gives me a big hug and whispers how much she loves me. I say the same back to her. Letting it out, though, makes me feel even more like crying. I manage to pull myself together, but only just.

Finally, it's time for people to take their seats for the fashion show. I quickly check with the stage manager that everything is ready to go. There's a mad frenzy going on of models getting their make-up touched up, designers sewing hems, shoes getting put on and taken off again. One of the models, a thin blonde-haired girl who looks barely older than I am, looks a bit ill and one of the assistants brings her a glass of water and some paracetamol.

'Um, is everything OK?' I ask worriedly.

'It's always like this,' the stage manager assures me. 'I'd say, go ahead and get started. We'll be ready.'

'OK,' I say. 'I will.'

A few minutes later, I'm standing in the wings of the stage, my insides flipping nervous somersaults. One of the crew gives a signal and the lights dim. A spotlight comes on, illuminating the catwalk. The music starts up and the screen flashes with hundreds of little dots in all colours that form a tunnel like a spaceship going into hyperspace. At the end of the tunnel, the logo of *The Polka Dot Shop* appears on screen. As I step out on stage, the music fades out. The microphone in my hand feels so heavy that I might drop it. I grip it for dear life, and hold it up to my mouth.

'Thank you all for coming today to the grand opening of *The Polka Dot Shop*.' I'm startled by the strength of my voice echoing through the theatre. 'A few months ago, I thought that the only thing that would save my mum's shop was a roll of bin bags and a skip.' I smile as a few people (luckily including Mum!) laugh at the joke. 'But since then, I've learned a thing or too, believe me.' I smile encouragingly at Mum, then turn back to face the crowd. 'I hope that you enjoy our fashion show and stick around afterwards to do a little shopping. I'm sure there will be something in *The Polka Dot Shop* that you'll love. Thank you, and enjoy.'

My knees feel like jelly as I step off the stage. The music blares in my ears as I hand the microphone to one of the stage hands and take my seat at the top of the catwalk. I spot Stevie's parents and Carrie's dad in the audience, sitting with Ms Cartwright and a few of the other teachers from school. But where are Stevie and Carrie? Are they backstage helping out? I watch the first model – wearing a vintage 'little black dress' from Hélène LeBoeff's collection – swagger to the end of the catwalk, pose, turn and walk back again. I scan the audience's faces looking for my friends, but I don't see them.

The show continues on, model after model, each outfit more interesting than the last. The fashion students have really outdone themselves, making unique pieces out of lots of the old fabric from *Eliza's Emporium*. There are smart women's suits made from old men's suits, little dresses and skirts made from denim, cardigans covered all over with fancy buttons, even a ballgown made from a collage of different fabrics with a collar made from costume jewellery. And interspersed are the classic pieces that we're selling from the 'Collection Belle Hélène' – Hélène LeBoeff's designer pieces. These stand out as the models saunter down the catwalk, sometimes next to a piece by a fashion student which was 'inspired' by it. We've also included some of the best consignment pieces. All in all, the catwalk is a whirlwind of lights, colours, and music—

But then, in the middle of the show, the lights in the theatre go out completely and the music cuts off. I gasp – this wasn't supposed to happen. I hear whispering in the audience. After a few seconds, the music comes back on – softly at first, and then louder. The spotlights begin to flash wildly. And then, from behind the screen, a figure emerges.

'Oh!' I clap my hand over my mouth as Carrie comes on to the stage and down the catwalk. Her hair has been slicked back, her face made up – and she looks absolutely gorgeous. She's wearing black wool trousers and Hélène's black-and-white houndstooth jacket, and heels which make her legs look long and slim. She comes to the end of the catwalk, turns and gestures to the stage. There's a hush and another figure comes out – moving slowly, one foot in front of the other. It's Stevie! She's wearing a silver lamé dress and silver ballet flats. In one hand she's carrying a little silver handbag studded with pink sequins. Her other arm is firmly gripping the arm of a figure in black – Thomas!

I cheer at the top of my lungs, my eyes shining. Thomas lets go of Stevie's arm and she takes the last three steps all by herself. I feel an unbelievable sense of joy and pride. Then he takes her arm again, and holds out his free hand and pulls me up on to the catwalk.

'You came!' I say.

But instead of saying so much as 'hello', Thomas leans in and gives me a kiss, full on the lips. In front of reporters, TV cameras, friends and family I turn the colour of a ripe tomato, and Stevie has to reach over and help steady *me* on my feet.

'You need to get backstage,' Thomas whispers into my ear. 'One of the models is sick.'

'What?' I say. But the three of them are already moving on, getting ready to turn round and walk back. I run down the catwalk to the wings.

Backstage, it's still complete chaos. I trip over Stevie's empty wheelchair and almost fall over the sick model I saw earlier, who's sitting off to one side with a bowl in her lap. The stage manager is busy trying to stuff one of the models into a Lanvin ballgown and do up the zip.

'Andy,' she says. 'Good, you're here. We need you for the grand finale. You're the only one small enough to fit into that dress.' She points to a rack – it's the polka-dot dress! Without a second thought, I get undressed, not caring who sees. One of the assistants helps me put the dress over my head. Another comes and touches up my make-up. Then, as the first is zipping me into the dress, someone else is twisting my hair and pinning it up and a third is shoving my feet into some high heels that feel about three sizes too small.

Stevie and Carrie come backstage after their big moment. Thomas helps Stevie into her chair, and then he looks up and his eyes lock with mine. And suddenly, at that moment, I'm both the me that is and the me that I could be, and I get the idea that he sees them both. And then he smiles, and I feel so flushed that I practically teeter over in the heels. An assistant takes me by the arm. 'It's time,' she says.

I walk out on to the stage. The lights swirl around me and the music vibrates through every cell in my body. Step by step I walk down the endless catwalk. I'm barely aware of the faces of the crowd, and every eye upon me. I get to the end and do a little twirl. The sparkles glitter and catch the light. And all around me, the noise of the crowd is deafening as the other models come out and join me on the catwalk, and people jump up from their seats to whistle and cheer. Stevie and

Carrie's parents are yelling at the top of their lungs, and Mum is standing at the back with Mr LeBoeff, smiling and crying at the same time. Ms Cartwright and the girls from school are on their feet cheering. And then, all I'm aware of is Stevie, Carrie and Thomas beside me at the end of the catwalk. Thomas helps Stevie to her feet, and the four of us stand there, shoulder to shoulder and take a bow.

'We did it,' I whisper to my friends. The lights are hot, the music is loud and the cheers are deafening. But as we stand there together smiling and squeezing hands, I know they hear me.

AUTHOR'S NOTE AND ACKNOWLEDGEMENTS

This book is dedicated to my three daughters, Eve, Rose and Grace, who have always loved dressing up, and will always be my princesses. I was inspired to write this book because I have a long-standing interest in vintage fashion, especially from the 1920s. Unfortunately, most of us normal-sized people can't fit into the sizes from back then, but I do love the care and craftsmanship that went into each piece. Whether or not you are into fashion, I hope that you have enjoyed Andy's journey and can find some inspiration in it.

I want to thank all of my readers, some of whom I've had the pleasure to meet over the last year on school visits. It is wonderful getting your reviews and feedback, and I love getting letters and emails from around the world.

While I was editing this book, we lost one of our greatest minds and champions of the human race, Stephen Hawking. However, I think we can take some comfort in the next generation – young people today – who can hopefully follow his lead to envision and create a better world.

I also want to thank my publisher, Chicken House, and the lovely editing staff who have helped make this book as good as it can be. I'd also like to thank my agent, Anna Power, and the members of my writing group who have been my loyal friends and critics for ten years now. Most of all, I'd like to thank my parents, Bruce and Suzanne, and Monica Yeo, and my partner Ian. Your support makes it all possible, and your love makes it worthwhile.

Laurel Remington

BIGFOOT, TOBIN & ME by MELISSA SAVAGE

When life gives you lemons, make lemonade.

Despite being named after her mum's favourite saying, there isn't much for Lemonade Witt to look forward to since her mother died – especially now she has moved to the wilds of Willow Creek.

Here, she meets an annoying boy called Tobin who, as head of Bigfoot Detectives Inc., is obsessed with finding the legendary beast. Reluctantly, she joins him in search of the elusive creature – but what they find instead is even better . . .

Paperback, ISBN 978-1-911077-18-3, £6.99 • ebook, ISBN 978-1-911077-51-0, £6.99

THE APPRENTICE WITCH by JAMES NICOL

Arianwyn fails her witch's assessment – instead of qualifying, she's declared an apprentice and sent to remote Lull in disgrace. Then her arch-enemy, mean girl Gimma, arrives on holiday determined to make her life a misery. But as a mysterious darkness begins to haunt her spells, Arianwyn realizes there's much more than her pride at stake . . .

'A charming tale of magic, bravery and friendship, reminiscent of Diana Wynne Jones.'
THE GUARDIAN

'The Apprentice Witch is entirely more charming, adventurous, and full of heart than a book has any right to be. Make no mistake: there's magic afoot.'
TRENTON LEE STEWART, AUTHOR

Paperback, ISBN 978-1-910655-15-3, £6.99 • ebook, ISBN 978-1-910655-62-7, £6.99

SKY CHASERS by EMMA CARROLL

Orphan Magpie can't believe her eyes when she sees a boy swept off his feet by a kite . . . or *something* that twists and dances in the wind. She goes to his rescue only to find herself dangling in the sky. The world looks so different from on high and suddenly Magpie knows what she wants – to be the first to fly in a balloon above the King and Queen of France.

'Sky Chasers is a real joy: funny, energetic and, as ever, brilliantly told.'
ABI ELPHINSTONE, AUTHOR

Paperback, ISBN 978-1-910655-53-5, £6.99 • ebook, ISBN 978-1-911077-39-8, £6.99